Hunger and Thirst and Other Plays

Other Works by Eugène Ionesco

Eugène Ionesco

HUNGER
AND
THIRST
and other plays

Translated from the French by Donald Watson

GROVE PRESS, INC. NEW YORK

Library of Congress Catalog Card Number: 73-79095

First Evergreen Edition, 1969

Third Printing

DISTRIBUTED BY RANDOM HOUSE, INC., NEW YORK

Manufactured in the United States of America

CONTENTS

HUNGER AND THIRST

Three Episodes

Characters

JEAN

MARIE-MADELEINE

AUNT ADELAIDE

FIRST KEEPER

SECOND KEEPER

THE BROTHER SUPERIOR

FIRST BROTHER (*or* BROTHER TARABAS)

SECOND BROTHER

THIRD BROTHER

FOURTH BROTHER

FIFTH BROTHER (*who will also play the part of the clown* TRIPP)

SIXTH BROTHER (*who will also play the part of the clown* BRECHTOLL)

MARTHE

I

THE FLIGHT

The Set

The stage represents a rather dark room. A door on the audience's left; an old chimney-piece in the rear wall, which is grey and somewhat dirty, with two windows or fan-lights high up. Facing the fireplace, a well-worn sofa. An old squat armchair front of stage, a cradle to one side. There is an old mirror on the right-hand wall. A plain table. A dilapidated chair. In the fireplace at the centre of the rear wall a blazing coal fire will appear and disappear, and later, a luminous garden.

JEAN *to Marie-Madeleine*]: I can't begin to understand you! Why come back to this place? We were better off where we were, in that new building. Windows all round, open to the sky . . . the light coming in from North, South, East, West, and all the other cardinal points. We used to go out on the gilded balcony. It was gold, remember? Space stretching all round us! No, no, I can't begin to understand. Why come and live here again?

MARIE: You used to complain there too! You said there was too much space. If it's not agoraphobia, it's claustrophobia!

JEAN: We were lucky to get away from this funereal ground-floor flat! It's not even that, it's a basement. As soon as we found a healthier place, we left.

MARIE: That's what you say now. But there, you didn't like the district. Here, at least, they don't rob you. They're respectable people. Small shopkeepers. They all know you and all our friends are still here.

JEAN *continuing his own line of thought*]: It's an absolute nightmare. *My* nightmare. I've always known it, since I was a child. I often woke up in the morning choking with fear. Because I've been dreaming of some ghastly house half sunk in the ground, half under water, oozing with mud. And look at this! Mud everywhere!

MARIE: It'll be all right. I'll dry it out. We'll have the plumbers in. They're easy to get hold of round here.

JEAN: Home sweet home! The water seeps into your boots, you shiver with cold, catch rheumatism and feel permanently out of sorts. Just what I wanted to avoid. I swore I'd never live in a basement again. Nightmares may be warnings, but I never thought they'd come true. Or perhaps I did have a vague idea. It *would* happen to *me*! I told you this before. I said I didn't want to come back.

MARIE: I didn't bring you here by force.

JEAN: I said I didn't want to come back. A lot of good that did me. The moment I let my mind wander, you take advantage. Sometimes it happens that I forget and think of other things. You can't hold everything in your mind all at the same time. The brain has its limits. So the moment I forget . . . And I swore I'd never come back. I just can't get over it. You must have known how I loathed the idea. But when my mind's on something else, you pounce. And while I'm dreaming of God-knows-what, you take me by the hand and ask me if I'll go with you. Absent-mindedly I say yes. You bring me here, with my head still in the clouds, and settle me in. You settle *us* in. All of a sudden I realise where I am. Where *you* had decided to bring me. The very place my nightmares had warned me not to go back to. And you knew, you knew, you knew . . .

MARIE: But we lived here a few years ago. For quite a long time. You weren't unhappy then.

JEAN: The place is not the same. You can see it's different now. In the old days, even if there wasn't much light, it *was* on the ground floor. Now it's sunk. It started sinking before we left. That's why we went, when the water seeped up through the floor. And to think there was no need for you to come back to this. Feel, the sheets are damp.

MARIE: I'll put warming-pans in the beds.

JEAN: The walls are damp! There's mildew round the skirting! It's dirty, it's greasy, it's cramped, and it's sinking all the time.

MARIE: You're making it up. What gives you the idea the house is sinking?

JEAN: Don't you ever notice anything?

MARIE: You always look on the black side. It's morbid. All imagination.

JEAN: It sticks out a mile! And it's always happening! Streets and towns, whole civilisations get swallowed up.

MARIE: It happens so slowly . . . so gradually . . . you don't realise . . . If it's as common as that we'll just have to put up with it. One day these buildings will be uncovered, disinterred. They'll see the light of day again and open out in the sun.

JEAN: Meanwhile we're sinking. This is the kind of place I hate.

MARIE: Most people live like this.

JEAN: They enjoy wallowing in the mire, they thrive on it. If they prefer the shadows or the dark, that's their lookout. But you could have spared *my* feelings. I suppose it's destiny. There's no escape for me. The only houses I like have roofs and walls you can see through. Or no roof and walls at all. Where the fresh air and the sunshine come

11

sweeping through in waves. Oh, for an ocean of sunshine!
... Oh, for an ocean of sky!

MARIE: But sometimes you used to say you wanted to leave the new house. That's why I started looking round.

JEAN: It was the last thing I had in mind. Unless we'd found another still more luminous, sky blue through and through. A house perched up in the mountains. There are such things, you know. Or even on some river. Not right *in* the river, but built out over the water, with flower-faces at the windows, flowers with their roots and stalks out of sight, just the top of them showing, flowers you can stretch out and touch. There are flowers that weep, of course, but also some that laugh. Why not choose flowers that shoot up in the world and smile?

MARIE: Gardens and houses like that are beyond our means, not within *our* reach.

JEAN: A wobbly armchair! Rotten old doors, a worm-eaten commode ...

MARIE: It's an antique.

JEAN: With mud in the drawers.

MARIE: That proves it's genuine. You're never satisfied!

JEAN: I know people who live on magical hilltops, glistening mountain peaks. And it's absurd how low their rents are. They pay less than we do, and some pay nothing at all.

MARIE: They inherited those from their parents. We didn't have their luck. But so long as I've a bed, a glimmer of light, and I've got you still at my side—it all seems beautiful.

JEAN: Darkness and gloom for us! And all I long for is the dawn!

MARIE: Some people have to live under bridges. You don't know when you're well off.

JEAN: They're the lucky ones! They've got streets and

squares, gardens and fields, and the seaside: the whole
world is theirs. You forget the rheumatism this house will
give us.

MARIE: Listen. This is a perfectly ordinary flat, with rooms,
beds, books and a kitchen. We're in our own home.

JEAN: . . . in sopping slippers and soaking wet clothes . . .

MARIE: I'll get them all dry in the little room next door.

JEAN: It always rains in the drying room. I won't live in this
place any more, I won't be consoled, or make the best of it.
I'm cold. There's no central heating!

MARIE: I'll warm the house with my heart.

JEAN: No electricity. Old oil lamps!

MARIE: I'll light it with my eyes.

JEAN: Some houses are like tombs. But if you can see the sky,
you forget. That's a consolation for living . . . and for dying.

MARIE: This is a house of habit.

JEAN: Looking forward to something is all that keeps me
going. Even the postman doesn't come down this street.

MARIE: So you'll get no more irritating letters! Nasty insulting letters and letters of thanks. All those begging letters.

JEAN: Not even the telephone.

MARIE: You can't stand the telephone. You wanted to get rid
of it!

JEAN: It's when I've got it, I want to get rid of it. When I
haven't got it, I've got to have it. You've got to have it
before you can get rid of it. Now I can't even get rid of the
telephone! There's nothing to look forward to, nothing to
do any more.

MARIE: You never could live like everyone else. For you,
there's always something missing!

JEAN: There always is. I only live in the hope something
fantastic will turn up. Even at school I could hardly wait
for Wednesdays to come round, and the Christmas

13

holidays. I'd look forward to the toys and the chocolates. I still remember the smell of the oranges, the tangerines. And then I lived in the hope that you would love me.

MARIE: And I do. So now, of course, you're after something else!

JEAN: Then, in the winter, I'd live in expectation of the spring. I'd dream of the summer holidays. And when they came I'd fix my thoughts on the autumn and going back to town. I've always longed for the snow, and the sea, and the mountains across the plain, and the clear water of the lakes. Above all I've looked forward to the ever-changing seasons. Here, it's a mixture of autumn and winter—one long grim season all the year round.

MARIE: It'll be quiet and restful. Nothing to disturb our peace.

JEAN: It's not peace I want, not mere contentment. It's boundless joy and ecstasy for me. And in these surroundings ecstasy is out. We've hardly been here more than twenty minutes. And now I look at you, you've aged already. Your first wrinkles. White hairs you didn't have before. Time goes faster than you think. Your head's drooping, a flower too heavy for its stalk.

MARIE: What's it matter how fast it goes? What's the difference, whether it takes ten minutes or an hour, a fortnight or a year? We all get there in the end.

JEAN: The ceiling will soon fall in. The plaster's crumbling. I can feel the weight on my shoulders already. Those patches on the walls are getting bigger. Is all this an image of time? Everything disintegrates before our very eyes.

MARIE: So long as I'm with you, I'm not afraid to die. If by taking one step I can touch your hand, or hear your voice from the next room when I call . . . then I'm happy. And *she's* here too [*she indicates the cradle*]. I know you love us.

14

Not enough, perhaps. Maybe you don't dare? Or you don't realise? But you *do* love us, I know you do. You've no idea the hold we have on your affections. Yes, in a way you do know. But not deep down. If only you could *really* know.

JEAN: Your hold on me is *great*. But the universe is greater, and what I need is greater still.

MARIE: She and I, we're all you need. One day, you'll understand. [*Aside:*] If only he knew how much he loves us!

JEAN: Who can make me forget I'm alive? I can't bear my own existence.

MARIE: You should get outside yourself more often and have a good look round. These walls with their patches of damp and mildew may appear old to you, but have you really *seen* them? Look at the beautiful shapes!

JEAN: Everything's so old.

MARIE *taking Jean by the hand to show him the marvels of the house*]: Not old. Antique. I thought you were a connoisseur. You can't really prefer that modern stuff! These shapes speak volumes, they're so expressive in their silence. I can see islands. Look: an ancient city, friendly faces to welcome us. Look again! Lips that smile, hands held out to us. And trees. You wanted flowers, you've got them on these walls, in lovely vases.

JEAN: However hard I look, all I can see is mildew, dilapidation . . . Oh yes, I can see . . . but not what you see. To me they look like bleeding carcasses, heads bowed in sorrow, frightened people dying, mutilated bodies, with no head, no arms, fabulous monsters, prostrate, in pain, gasping for breath . . .

MARIE: They must be harmless then, not dangerous any more.

JEAN: Their sufferings have been handed on to us. And there,

15

you see the head of that old man? Yes, an old Chinaman, with a wrinkled face. How sad he looks, in his coolie hat. He's sick, of course... He's being attacked by rats! They're up on his shoulders, they're going to devour his face!

MARIE: You're wrong: he's a serene old man, he's beaming at us, he's going to speak to us.

JEAN: And the rats on his shoulders, ready to pounce?

MARIE: Pet rats: on their hindlegs, gently sniffing his face.

JEAN: His chest is covered in blood from the gaping wounds.

MARIE: Why no, dear, it's not that at all! It's a red cloak he's wearing, with gold braid on it . . . I'm sure he's the wise man of the house, its guardian. Old houses are full of moving memories. All the ghostly tenants of the past live on: nobody dies.

[*Enter* AUNT ADELAIDE *through the door on the audience's left. Before she enters, she can be seen arriving in the mirror. She comes in and sits down quite naturally on the old sofa. She is dressed in long veils, which give her the look of a great lady in decline, poverty-stricken, almost a down-and-out.*]

JEAN: Aunt Adelaide!

MARIE: Oh yes, it's Aunt Adelaide!

ADELAIDE *she seems annoyed*]: I've come to pay you a visit.

JEAN *to Aunt Adelaide*]: I can't think *why* you've come, Aunt Adelaide. What do you want with us?

ADELAIDE: I bother you, don't I? Upset you?

JEAN: You don't upset us, we're fond of you, you know we are. [*Aunt Adelaide shrugs her shoulders and laughs bitterly.*] You don't appear to believe me, but it's true.

MARIE: She doesn't believe you. She can't understand you. Even in the past, she never really understood. It's not her fault.

ADELAIDE: I understand everything. Sometimes I pretend I don't, so you'll think I'm stupid. But I understand all

16

right. I understand everything.

JEAN: Then you should realise you've no business to be here, sitting on that sofa.

ADELAIDE: I have come to pay you a visit. Is this how you welcome me? Like this? The family never appreciated me. No-one's a prophet in his own family. Strangers respect me. *They* kiss my hand and say "Please don't go. *Do* stay to dinner". But I always say no. I don't upset *them*, I only bother *you*. You hate me because I'm famous. Since that's the way you feel, I shall leave. [*She stands up, then sits down again.*] No, I'm not hungry, thank you. I never drink coffee. Never touch wine. Never, never, never. I've always led a sober life. I never gave up my work. I was an inspiration to my husband, the great doctor. Most of the treatises on medicine and surgery that bear his name were in fact written by me. He owed his brilliant career to me. And I never told a soul, not a soul. I'm so modest. Still, the other professors knew. They guessed *I* was the author. They never *said* so. It was a *tacit* understanding. Conveyed by winks, and signs and insinuations. I used to tell them he wrote his books himself, so as not to betray him. His colleagues, hospital consultants and members of the Medical Council, would look at me and smile. I'd smile back. Oh yes, I'd return their smiles. They were handsome men. They used to come courting me. And it still goes on, even now. I get so pestered by my admirers, I often have to lock my door. They write me letters I tear into little pieces and throw in the wastepaper basket. I don't wish to marry again.

MARIE: She hasn't changed!

JEAN *to Aunt Adelaide*]: When they're chasing you, these admirers, where do they find you?

ADELAIDE: At home, of course, in my own home . . . If I

17

don't let them in, they watch for me on the stairs. Then I have to go out by the servants' door. One or two will be lying in wait for me there as well. Yes, they come to my house.

JEAN: Think carefully, Aunt Adelaide! Where is your home?

ADELAIDE: Where it always was.

JEAN: Where's that?

ADELAIDE: My flat. I've been living there for years. You know!

JEAN: Don't you remember? You left it.

MARIE *to Jean*]: Be quiet!

JEAN *to Aunt Adelaide*]: There's been another family there for some time now.

MARIE *to Jean*]: Don't remind her of *that*.

ADELAIDE: Poor unfortunate people who had nowhere to go! They were out on the streets. They kept me a room I can use whenever I like. I've the key of the house to prove it. Look! This one. In the daytime I work, I give courses at the University. Then I go to the library to study. No need to show my credentials. They know me. In the evening I attend lectures put on for the staff. Then, tired but happy, I go home for the night. If my lodgers wake up to welcome me, I tell them to go back to bed. They appreciate that. "Can we get you anything, Madame?" they ask. "Anything you need, Doctor?" "Don't worry about me", I say, "don't you worry about me! I don't want to be a nuisance when I come home. It'll never do to wake the baby!" I step out of my shoes and tactfully tiptoe off to my own little nest. I always consider other people, and never think of myself. Quietly I close the door and then I get into bed. Eight hours of sleep. I drop off straightaway. Next day I wake up fresh as a daisy, and carry on as before. You know that little room of mine, don't you?

18

At the end of the passage, on the left? That's where you used to sleep when you were small. The window looks out on the Boulevard where the Metro runs above ground.

JEAN: It's not true. You should face the facts. That story's not true at all.

MARIE *to Jean*]: Don't cross her ... There is *some* truth in what she says.

ADELAIDE *to Jean*]: You used to like to hear the trains go by. The rumbling would rock you off to sleep. Your mother always sent you to stay with me when she meant you to have a bath. There was no bathroom at your place. The apartments you lived in were never very grand. I paid the rent and I couldn't afford a larger flat. You weren't at all pleased. But it's not that I was mean, I had too many commitments. I used to support the whole family: *your* mother, *my* father and mother. You used to live with your grandparents, the two of you. Wasn't I the one who paid for everything? Your uncle was a consul, always abroad. *He* didn't look after you. And your poor mother! Oh dear! Your father had gone off and left her. She said it was all my fault, that he'd divorced her because of me. Are these lies I'm telling you now?

JEAN: I did sleep in that room when I was small. Often. And later too, when I came to Paris.

ADELAIDE: You see.

JEAN: Yes, it's true. In the evenings I used to lean out the window to watch the trains go by. They were all lit up, and you could see the heads of the people inside.

ADELAIDE: Then why do you lie? You see, I am telling the truth, I'm not mad.

JEAN: There's one thing that *isn't* true. Come on, make an effort, think! Do you really go home every evening to sleep?

ADELAIDE: Every evening. Yes, Jean.

JEAN: To your own home? And stay with the people there? They really see you come in? And you talk? Answer me!

ADELAIDE *evading an answer to the question*]: I don't walk about dressed in this way, like a pauper, just to go begging. I've lost all my money. Given everything away. To everybody. But I've not been abandoned. I *am* being helped. Other people help me: *other* people are grateful to me . . . not the family. Oh, the family! I ask nothing of the family . . .

JEAN: That's not the point.

ADELAIDE *continuing*]: . . . When I go out for an evening stroll, it's because I need the air. When I hold out my hand by the entrance to the big department stores and stand for hours pretending to queue up at the bus-stops, it's not to beg for alms. Oh no! I don't want charity. It's so I can observe the passers-by: I write books . . .

JEAN: *We've* never seen them.

MARIE *to Jean*]: Let her talk . . . It does her good.

ADELAIDE: *You* never see anything. Well, it's a fact. Books about life, about the streets, about society, and morality to-day, about our schools. I write the true biographies of famous men. Heads of state. I know them personally. They've explained everything to me and I'm the only one who knows their secrets. I make out reports on scientific subjects. Only yesterday I read a paper to the Institute. They said I was brilliant. You didn't come, of course, you or your wife. The professors from the Sorbonne, the College of France and the Academy of Science all turned up in force.

JEAN: You know quite well you're inventing all this. But that's not the question.

ADELAIDE: You'll both find out one day who I am. Then you'll be sorry. You don't *want* to believe me. Look at the decorations I've had!

JEAN: I tell you that's not the point. Look here, Aunt Adelaide, I'm asking you to make an effort. Give me an answer: yesterday evening, did you really sleep at home? Were you in your flat?

MARIE *to Jean*]: You'll never get a straight answer.

ADELAIDE: I always have a good night's rest. I work all day, so I *need* rest. I sleep like a top. I'm not ill. I'm in very good health.

JEAN: Right. Where have you come from now?

ADELAIDE: From home . . . from my *home*, I tell you. I got up a bit later than usual. It's a holiday today, it's Sunday.

MARIE: Maybe she pretends not to know. Maybe she's forgotten.

JEAN: You never can tell with her. We never could. She's always been like this. Sometimes she knows she's playing a part, sometimes she doesn't. And at times she tells the truth. In a way what she says is true, surprising as it may seem. She's often surprised us. You can never be sure with her.

ADELAIDE: These decorations I've been awarded, you don't think they're genuine, do you? I have the citations in my bag. I'll show you. Though I didn't bring them all. I've got dozens of medals and crosses and ribbons.

MARIE: We believe you. There's no need to show us!

ADELAIDE: Oh, but I must! Look! I've got some here! [*She takes from her bag a handful of medals and ribbons:*] Look, children! Now you can see who I am! [*She puts the decorations back in her bag, which she closes again.*]

JEAN: You always change the subject. But you know what I'm getting at. Remember? You set your house on fire. Set light to the drawing-room curtains. The fire brigade had to turn out.

ADELAIDE: My next-door neighbour did it to spite me.

JEAN: How could she get in?

ADELAIDE: She'd had a key made. She spies on me, I see her peeping behind the curtains. As soon as I go out, she runs in. If I've any flowers around, she pulls them about. But she's cunning: she tears off the petals just one at a time. Then the flowers die. I have to drop them in the dustbin. Once, when I'd had a skirt made for me, I went out for a quarter of an hour, so I could come back and catch her. But she saw me, and got away in time. I went in and there was the skirt on the bed, where I'd left it. But it wasn't lying in the same position. I knew she'd been up to something. She'd put another skirt in its place, an identical one, the same colour. But made of nettles. She'd dyed the nettles to match the skirt. If you don't believe me, just look at her when she walks past! Wicked creature! You'll see! It's the *real* skirt she's wearing.

JEAN: You lost all your furniture. So you had no bed. It was destroyed in the fire. They took you off to hospital.

ADELAIDE: That's a lie. You're on *their* side. I've many enemies, who want their revenge. So they persecute me and tell stories about me.

JEAN: What have they got against you?

ADELAIDE: It's not true. I've never been ill. Never, never been ill. I know the chief consultant in the hospital. He's an old friend of mine. Since he was a student. I was his "Professor". He warned me. He said: "You have enemies, Madame. They envy you." I've never been in hospital. Do you think I'm mad?

JEAN: When you left the hospital, where did you go?

ADELAIDE: I wasn't in the hospital.

JEAN: Yes, you were. Do you want me to say where they took you next?

22

MARIE *who has gone to sit near the cradle, interrupting her rocking for a moment*]: Don't tell her that!

ADELAIDE *standing up*]: You're both making a mistake. I'm not a ghost. Look! I move, I speak, I can talk, I have arms, I have legs, I can walk. Anywhere I choose. I have a beautiful bosom, in spite of my years. [*She opens her bodice, takes off her brassière and shows her breasts:*] Your wife can look too. Are hers as lovely as mine? That's why they came courting me. These are not the breasts of a ghost. My thighs are beautiful too. My flesh is firm. Almost too muscular: gymnastics, you know. To keep fit.

MARIE: You'd better go, Aunt Adelaide. Calm yourself! Cover yourself! [*Adelaide covers herself again with her cloak.*] If I ask you nicely: please go now! You can come back another time. We'll invite you to lunch.

ADELAIDE: I've got blood in my veins. Ghosts haven't. Look! Lovely red blood! [*After taking off her hat, overloaded with artificial flowers and grapes, she takes out a knife and slits her skull:*] That's my blood flowing!

JEAN: Seems true enough. It's flowing all right.

ADELAIDE *to Marie-Madeleine, indicating her opened skull*]: Put your hand here, you'll see! [*Marie-Madeleine refrains. To Jean:*] Feel! There's your proof. You've never believed me, always accused me of lying. [*Adelaide has taken Jean's hand almost by force and made him touch the wound. Jean withdraws his hand and looks at Marie-Madeleine.*]

JEAN *looking at his hand*]: It's not real blood. It's not liquid. And then it's too dark to be blood. It's like jelly. Gelatine! Sticky! And it doesn't stain! [*He looks at his hand*]: A moment ago I had it all over my fingers: now it's vanished. But if it was powdered blood . . . you'd have to . . . blow it away . . . No, Aunt Adelaide, it's definitely not real blood. You're trying to mislead us.

23

MARIE *to Jean*]: She's giving another performance.

ADELAIDE: I am an artist, but this is not a performance. You're mad, the two of you. Poor things. You've always, always, always, accused me of lying. I'm going to see my professors. They respect me, they do, they believe me. *They* don't tell me I'm mad. They *know* I'm not. I shall never visit you again. Never. I'm sorry. Not for you. But for the baby in her cradle. In the whole family she's the only one I love. It's for her sake I come, in spite of your jibes. [*She goes out. For a few moments you can still see her reflection in the mirror.*]

JEAN *while she is leaving*]: It's a shame! Anyway, I didn't kill Aunt Adelaide!

MARIE: How *could* you have killed her? You weren't even at the funeral!

JEAN: It's only *here* she's able to find us.

MARIE: She won't come back again now, when she's realised what's happened to her. Still, you shouldn't have let her go in that condition, without a friendly word. You get so worked up. Why aren't you more tolerant? You never get on with anyone these days.

JEAN: She's not herself any more. Why do people like that come and visit us here? Why?

MARIE: Don't puzzle your head about that! Think about her too, and the state she's in! You should have been more sympathetic, more understanding. She's a near relation. Don't we all avoid facing facts? You should have tried to explain. But now forget it! You're shivering, you're cold. Come and sit here. No . . . Let's walk up and down together.

JEAN: I really can't stay in this house any more. I can't stand it . . .

MARIE *tired*]: I know, I know . . . You're neurotic. There's a cure for that.

24

JEAN: I see things as they are. And that's *in*curable.

MARIE: Even if you do have your reasons, ignore them! Forget them! Take life as it comes! You always want to do something about it. Don't! Shall I open the drawers of this old desk? Look at these old photos, a pageant from the past, people from the last century, a thousand years ago, photos of every period, from Ancient Times till now, all the people who ever lived here. What kind faces they've got! The whole of the past is here.

JEAN: I don't care for other people's memories.

MARIE: A photo of you as a child . . .

JEAN: My own are a dead-weight already: like these walls, or this ceiling weighing us down.

MARIE: We'll bear it, as best we can, on our shoulders . . .

JEAN: If only I could have those other memories!

MARIE: Which ones?

JEAN: The memories we've forgotten. No! I don't mean those. Different ones . . . The memories of a life I never lived. No, that's not what I mean: memories I've never had, impossible memories . . .

MARIE: You're asking too much.

JEAN: That's all I ask.

MARIE: Your teeth are chattering, you're shivering. I'll light the fire.

[*A chimney-piece appears against the back wall, on the right, with a blazing fire; or in the mirror.*]

JEAN: No, don't! Put it out! I can't stand the sight of that woman in the flames. Look at her hair! That's how I always see her, desperate, holding out her arms, in agony. Then she vanishes in smoke and leaves a heap of ashes at my feet. But next time the fire is lit, there she is again, rising like a phoenix, an eternal reproach. And never, never have I dared to brave the flames. [*Addressing*

25

the woman he sees in the flames:] Yes, I know you're frightened,
I know you are in pain. If only I could help you. But I
can't. Forgive me.

MARIE *to the imaginary woman in the flames*]: It's not his fault,
my dear. He couldn't save you. He was ready to attempt
the impossible. But that was more than impossible. It's not
his fault. Believe me, it's not his fault! Go away! Please,
please go away! [*The chimney-piece and the flames disappear.
To Jean*:] Is that better?

JEAN: This house has weird visitors.

MARIE: You'll get used to it. It doesn't frighten *me*. Now
you're cold again.

JEAN: I'm cold. And I'm too hot. And I'm hungry. I'm
thirsty too. I've lost my appetite. No taste left for anything.

MARIE: You'll get used to it, I tell you. I'll help you, you'll
see. You can make a nest out of anything and find refuge
in nostalgia. Feed on desire and quench your thirst with
hope. Wishful thinking's a waste of time. Harsh memories
can be muted, made a source of entertainment. Turn
despair into sadness: sadness into regret. Feed on your
melancholy. Parents and friends who are dead can live
on in the mind, remain in constant touch. They're a
world in themselves. A restful night absorbs the shadows
of the past. The sun will shine today, the sky will be clear
tomorrow: if you wish hard enough. If your eyesight's
good you can see through walls that block your view of
the horizon . . . Turn your failures into rest and relaxation.
Look forward in the morning to the evening that brings
peace: without fail it will come. At night dream of the
spectacle of dawn. That too will come. And so it is with
all things.

JEAN: I have such a feeling of emptiness!

MARIE: Come to terms with it, and find fulfilment!

26

JEAN: Impossible! Sentimentality! That's not the answer!
[*Marie-Madeleine sits down, with her back to the audience, still rocking the child in the cradle. Jean is standing up, facing the audience, on the spectators' left, not far from the door. Both characters are talking to themselves.*]

JEAN: I won't be frightened! No, I'll never be scared again! I don't care who comes to haunt me in this subterranean slum. I'm not afraid of these eccentrics any more! I know who sends them, Marie-Madeleine, I know! They won't catch me, never again, they've lost their power over me. They'd like me to be bitten by remorse, crippled by repentance, they want pity to draw blood from my heart: but I know their game and I'm not playing any more. Their teeth are not so keen, their claws no longer tear my flesh. I've done away with pity and regret. I've killed all feeling for the sufferings of mankind. I've shared the torments of my fellows far too long: I've cast that millstone off. I'll be as light as air and celebrate my newfound liberty in song. I'll drown all cares and dance for joy.

MARIE: We'll fix the place up. I'll repair that old desk and re-cover the sofa. [*To the child she is rocking:*] Go bye-byes, sleepy-pies, grow big and strong, sleepy-eyes. [*Then, to herself:*] If only he knew what he wanted! What he wants is already within his grasp, staring him in the face. Where else does he hope to find it? You see, Jean, she's smiling, soon she'll be able to talk.

JEAN: I can't stand the sight of myself any more. An ugly reflection in a cracked mirror.

MARIE: If he could *really* see himself, he'd know how beautiful he is. He'd stop hating himself. I've known him so long, since the world began. And I'm joined to him for all eternity. Why do these bonds seem like chains to him? All I want is to call his name and hear him answer. He's there,

27

and that's enough.

JEAN: I'll turn a deaf ear to appeals for help, ignore the grey voices of resignation.

MARIE: We'll bar the door and put a new lock on, with a nice big key, to keep us safe from burglars and disaster.

JEAN: I'll go away.

MARIE: We won't travel any more. Where else can we go? We've reached our destination. Outside this house, outside us two, outside us three, anywhere else is nowhere.

JEAN: I'm so tired . . . fatigue holds me back, my legs are like jelly, my head's like lead. I'm frightened to death again.

MARIE: I've hung the baby's nappies up to dry. And her little dress. Isn't it sweet? It's your birthday today. Every day's a birthday. The anniversary of something. I've brought you some pretty pictures, chocolate and cigarettes. Every day I bring you a heart new-born.

JEAN: Every day's a birthday. Every day reminds me of old age, every morning fills me with despair. Soon I shall disintegrate. Lassitude can kill and so can fear.

MARIE: If you're sick with fear, you're scared wherever you are. When he's far away and all alone, he'll be more frightened than ever. And he wants to go roaming around like a mad thing! He's got all he needs, he's got everything here, but he wants to go roaming about!

JEAN: Is it too late? I'll conquer my fears. Is this the last chance, is there still time? Everyone knows my address. If I stay, they'll surround the house and mount guard: at any moment they'll be here to stop me going. I don't want to be like them, I won't get stuck in a rut or just drift along like the rest. Their destiny's not mine, my life is somewhere else.

MARIE *to the child*]: Yes, darling! Yes, my little pink baby! He loves you. He loves us both, more than words can tell.

28

JEAN: Fatigue wonders what's the point of going. Old age suggests I stay where I'm well off. Caution warns I'll do myself no good, and goodness says I'll do harm to others. And duties? Obligations? Deep-rooted affections? And reason? They won't catch me with their arguments. They bore me stiff with their "experience". Because *they* never dared, they want *me* to stick in the mud. I'm meant for something better.

MARIE: I love you, you love me, you love her. We love one another so much. You'll always be here, always always be. Even if you go to the ends of the world, even if you *think* you're alone, I am and shall be with you. But will you be able to go? Will he be able to go? He's not used to walking. He over-estimates his strength, he doesn't know how tired he'll feel. He can't last out two hundred yards on foot. He's out of training. Not to speak of the hardships and the dangers.

JEAN: I'll take my boots, my stick, and my hat. I need healthy surroundings. The clean air will wake me up, give me back my strength. I must have mountain air, somewhere like Switzerland, a hygienic country where nobody dies. A land where the law forbids you to die. When you enter that land, you must make a declaration. A promise not to die. You have to sign it. Death is not allowed. Attempt it, you get a fine and a prison sentence. That way you're forced to exist.

MARIE: If he's set his heart on a change of air, he might as well go. But he'd better take his big greatcoat. Don't get cold, don't catch a chill, be careful! Spring only lasts a few hours. And summer a couple of days. Then comes the dreary season, stretching endlessly over the plains.

JEAN: I'll get some colour back in my cheeks. Everything will turn green again. I'll turn green again too.

29

MARIE: I was thinking of having the house done up in gay colours. We'll be so nice and cosy in our armchairs once they've been renovated. For coffee, and a snooze . . . and a baby in arms. And me. Not forgetting me.

JEAN: Once upon a time I was strong, I was a great weight-lifter. What's the increase, as you grow older, in your own weight in pounds?

MARIE: But how is it he won't put down roots? Why doesn't he want to be like an old wall, or an oak, covered in moss or ivy? An old oak with its roots deep in the earth. A tree doesn't move around. Why is he so unhappy? Why is he so obtuse? It's moving around that upsets things.

JEAN: If I'm to harden my heart, I'd better steep it in the sorrows of others. I am tired. What an effort to move my arm. Or even my thumb! Chin up! Fresh unfailing energy will bring me back to life.

MARIE: He thinks this house is a tomb. Why does he get in a state? All houses are tombs. In ours it's hot in winter, cool in summer, nice and warm in the spring.

JEAN: I'll loosen the knots and slip my bonds. I'll bury my past, lest it buries me. I banish memory. I'll keep just enough to know who I am, and remember only this: that I am nothing but myself and must myself remain.

MARIE: Were you really able to pull up the roots, my love? Can you really tear out the roots of love, the love you feel, the love you have for us? Could you uproot love without leaving a wound, could you tear love out, that love in your heart? Could you rip it out, from your heart that love, that love that lies in your heart . . . What garden is it you hope to find? You can't really go. You know *we're* here, you know *I'm* here. You're joking aren't you, you're staying aren't you, pretending aren't you? From your heart you cannot tear out love, the wrench would be too great, no-one could heal that wound. You can't pull up the roots of love, you can't tear love from your heart, the love in your heart, from your heart. It's a game you're playing, isn't it?

[*Jean, standing on the audience's left, listens facing the auditorium. Marie-Madeleine, seated, rocking the cradle, with her back to the auditorium. At the end of this kind of refrain Marie-Madeleine is chanting Jean turns round and tiptoes out behind the back wall.*]

MARIE: Are you there? Where are you? [*A game of hide-and-seek. Jean reappears at the other side of the stage.*]

JEAN: Here I am!

MARIE: I knew you were there, I saw you. [*Jean disappears again*]. Where are you going? Where are you? Now, that's enough! [*Reappearance of Jean, or of his head.*]

JEAN: I'm in the house.

MARIE: Of course you're in the house.

JEAN: I'm in the house.

MARIE: I know you are. Where are you? [*She stands up.*]

JEAN *who has disappeared*]: In the house.

MARIE: Don't hide! [*She looks round for him.*]

JEAN's voice: Look for me, I'm not far away! Look, I'm quite close!

MARIE *shouting*]: Well, come closer, come on now! Come and look at baby in her cradle! Come and see how she smiles! [*Jean reappears behind a piece of furniture.*]

JEAN: Here I am! I'm coming! [*He disappears.*]

MARIE: Where's here?

JEAN *appearing at some other place on the stage, where you can only see him from the waist up*]: Here!

MARIE *seeing him*]: Why have you got your hat on? Why have you put on those gloves? Why are you getting into that old jacket? What's that old coat of yours doing over your arm?

31

It's got no buttons. I'll have to sew them on.

JEAN: Here I am! Here I am! [*Continual disappearances and appearances.*]

MARIE: Stop dressing up! Take off that balaclava! Come along, my love, listen! Don't hide your face behind that black handkerchief! Come along, please!

JEAN *disappearing*]: I'm coming!

MARIE: Where are you?

JEAN's voice: Here! Can you still see me? Here!

MARIE: Show yourself, Jean!

JEAN's voice: Cooee! Cooee!

MARIE: Stop playing hide-and-seek! Still the same stupid old games! You might invent some new ones, you're not a child any more!

JEAN's voice: Here I am! Here I am! Cooee!

MARIE: That's enough, I tell you! That's quite enough now! All this playing about upsets me. I can't help it, it gets on my nerves! Come along now, come and look at her, come and sit down beside me! She wants you, she's trying to say Dada!

JEAN's voice: Here I am!

MARIE *looking for him in the room*]: Jean! Cooee! Jean, I'm tired. Stop playing about! Where are you?

JEAN's voice: Here! Cooee!

MARIE: Cooee!

JEAN's voice: Cooee!

MARIE: Now Jean, dear, that's enough! Please stop this game!

JEAN's voice: Here I am! Cooee!

[*Marie-Madeleine is frantically looking for him, behind the furniture, behind the walls, at the door. She appears and disappears leaving the stage empty for a moment, while you can still hear their "cooees". She reappears and disappears behind a piece*

32

of furniture: once or twice more you can see Jean's head appearing when Marie-Madeleine is no longer visible on stage. She looks for him everywhere, even in the cupboard. She swings round suddenly in the hope of catching him, as though he were there beside her, invisible. Distracted, she starts off all over again, still shouting her "cooees" and weeping.]

MARIE: I'm trying to find you! Yes, I'm trying so hard, really I am! Do you want me to come and touch you? Now I'm really getting cross! Come on now, where are you? Come along! Come along! Will you come! Be sensible! Cooee! Cooee! You might at least tell me if I'm getting warm!

JEAN's voice: Cooee! Cooee!

MARIE *searching*]: Jean, my little dear, my darling, my Jeannot! Are you there? Are you here? Cooee! Cooee! Are you behind the wardrobe? In the cupboard, the sideboard, the passage, the kitchen? Over in *this* corner? Over in *that* one? Where are you? Tell me! Where are you? Cooee!

JEAN's voice: Cooee!

MARIE: He must be here if he answers. Please, Jean! *Please!*

JEAN's voice *very distant*]: Cooee!

MARIE: No, you'll never be able to tear love from your heart, the love that binds us, you and me. [*Chanting away, she is still looking for him in the most unlikely places.*] From your heart you cannot tear this love, you can't tear love from your heart. This love from your heart you cannot tear, you can't tear it out, you can't rip it away. Cooee! Cooee! Which room are you in? Not in the kitchen, nor in the bathroom, or under the bed either. Which chest have you climbed into? Show yourself! Please! You'll get all dirty and hurt yourself if you're up the chimney! Cooee! Cooee! Don't be such a child! Where are you? Behind the door?

33

No. Are you calling me from the next house?

JEAN's voice *very far away*]: Cooee!

MARIE: Is his voice coming from the cellar? Are you in the cellar? Is he on the roof? Is his voice reaching me from the roof? Cooee! Cooee! No, he can't tear this love from his heart. He can't rip it out without leaving a wound, this love, this love so deep in his heart, he can't tear it up from his heart. He's not gone! He's not gone, I can hear him. He's answered. Cooee, Jean! Cooee! [*Wildly she searches the whole stage, rather like a marionette, a bit like a child.*] That's enough, for goodness' sake! The baby's holding her arms out to you. Answer! Cooee! Answer, can't you! Answer! Cooee! Answer! *Please*, I can't find you anywhere. I used to know all your old hiding-places, but not this one. You can't have disappeared, you can't have gone out. I'll go on playing just for one minute more, I don't mind looking for one minute more, but at least let me hear your voice! Say Cooee! Cooee! [*She goes on looking for him under the table, behind the chair, under the tablecloth, under the chair, under the sideboard, in the drawer. She uses her spectacles and a magnifying glass. She is panic-stricken and goes on calling:*] Cooee! Cooee! You answered just now. Jean, you can't have gone out, can you? You can't have gone away, can you? You'd have told me, wouldn't you? Answer! Cooee! I can hear him. No. I can't hear him. This is a cruel game. Do you understand what I'm saying? Can you hear what I'm telling you? This is a cruel game. Much too cruel! [*She goes on looking for him automatically, with less and less conviction, not looking too hard, slowing the pace down.*] No, he can't tear this love from his heart. [*She goes out for a few seconds and while she is chanting this sort of refrain, Jean appears. He violently tears from his heart a branch of briar rose, his face screwed up with pain, wipes the drops of blood from his fingers on his shirt; puts the branch down on the*

34

table, carefully buttons his jacket and then tiptoes out. He disappears behind the back wall. As he tears the branch out, he says:)

JEAN: Now for it! . . . Ouch! . . . Way above the wintry valleys . . . Ouch! . . . And the fields . . . Ouch! And the hills . . . On the highest spur . . . *there* stands the princess's palace . . . in the middle of a sunlit park. Ouch! . . . From there you can see the ocean meet the sky . . . I must go . . .

MARIE's voice *at the same time, rather muffled*]: This love he cannot from his heart tear out, from your heart you cannot tear out love, the love in your heart can't be ripped away . . .

MARIE *re-appearing*]: How can he have disappeared? He's not there! Not there and not here either. He's just not here! How empty the house is. What a great emptiness! It was bound to happen some day, of course. I knew it. He was too fond of playing that game. He just got carried away. We often used to play. And I warned him what it would lead to, though we always came together in the end. I'll call, I'll call him again. Cooee! Cooee! I can't play this game all alone, you need two to play. He used to try and find me too. But now I'm all alone. And that's why I can't find him. That's it, of course. Of course it is. Which way can he have gone? How can he have slipped away? The doors and windows were shut. [*She goes to the rear of the stage and comes back.*] No, I don't want to go through that mouldy passage again, full of spiders and woodlice. Everyone will ask what was wrong with him. A hopeless case of nostalgia. That's what I'll say. But I'll go on looking, in every nook and cranny, though I know he's not here any more. I won't be able to stop myself. I'll reach out to touch him, but there'll be no head on his pillow. Each morning I'll take him his dressing-gown. Though I know he won't be having his bath. How frightened he'll be, wherever he is. He's not the type to go wandering off through those grey deserted plains. How can he have left me? How ever did he make up his mind? Where did he find the courage to go off on his own? [*She sees the branch on the table, takes it in her hand and looks at it.*] He really has torn out the flower of love, pulled it up by the roots. How can he have ripped it out of his heart, how can he from his heart have ripped it? Poor Jean! How he must suffer! My poor little Jean's been hurt. He's leaving a trail of blood, behind him on the road. [*She sits down near the cradle which she starts rocking, her back turned to the audience. In her other hand she is holding the branch.*] We're alone now, little one. How can I lose the habit I've got of touching him, expecting him. Can I get used to not hearing his answering voice? [*She takes up the refrain again:*] If you could tear this love from your heart, if you could tear this away, if you could tear this love from your heart, from your heart, from your heart . . . [*The back wall, which she is looking at, vanishes. You can see a garden: trees in blossom, tall green grass, a very blue sky.*] Oh! [*She half rises, then sits down again. By some movement of her shoulders and her back she must convey to the audience the wonder she herself feels. Then, on the left of this landscape, which is also on the audience's left, you can see a silver ladder appear, hanging in the air, the top of it out of sight. The joy and astonishment of Marie-Madeleine, who is contemplating the landscape, is still conveyed, perceptibly but discreetly, by certain movements of the shoulders. She stands up very quietly:*] He didn't know *that* was here! He couldn't have seen *that*. I thought the *garden* was here. I suspected it was. Though I wasn't absolutely sure. If only he'd seen, if only he'd known! If he'd had a little patience, he wouldn't have gone, he wouldn't have left us behind!

CURTAIN

II

THE RENDEZVOUS

The Set

A terrace that appears to be hanging in mid-air. A dark sky. Later, when Jean arrives, the sky will clear. The light, however, will be cold, an empty brilliance, without shadow and without sun. In the background and as far as possible all round, arid mountains. Jean enters.

JEAN: What wonderful light! I've never seen anything so pure! Those mountains could seem too stark. But I like clarity. [*Discreet appearance, on the right, of the First Keeper, with cap and moustache.*] Good morning. I love the light in this part of the world. I like the dust too. These stone buildings and the altitude. Especially after roaming through so many wet countries: gloomy plains, marshland and rain. See how these mountains stand out against the sky, they look almost alive. It's all so new to me.

1st KEEPER: Have you travelled down from the North?

JEAN: From the North? Well, you know, really I'm not too sure . . . I've no sense of direction. Countries where it rains anyway. Dark and dusky lands. This is the kingdom of light.

1st KEEPER: I suppose so. Rather an empty brilliance, though. A bit bleak, perhaps. If that's what you're after, help yourself.

JEAN: This is the entrance to the museum, isn't it? Are there still lots of visitors?

1st KEEPER: At the moment it's not the season. Do you want to go in?

JEAN: Not just yet. I'm waiting for her.

1st KEEPER: It's not the first time you've been?

JEAN: No, that's why I'm here. When you've seen it once, you can't help coming back. What a brilliant idea: to have your museum on this vast plateau at the highest point. When she's arrived, we'll both go in and see the statues. All those amazing rooms I promised to show her. This domain is the finest in the world. The situation's sublime. There's no other word. To think I can show her this land where once I came bewildered and alone. To think I can be here with her now. Happiness uplifts me . . . No, it's more than that, it's a rising tide of irresistible joy, a great wave that sweeps through me and makes the desert fertile. Have I really been here before? Of course, but I can't tell you when. The actual date escapes me. Did I come here before? Or did I only imagine this place? Yet somehow I seem to have been brought here. Yes, of course I was, I was here before and *she* wasn't able to come. Now I remember. All those impressions lost in the dark night of memory are coming back to me one by one. They weren't gone for good. Now they're emerging, each one clearer than the last. As if the waters of oblivion had washed them clean. Oh, it's beautiful, it's magnificent! As dazzling as it was the first time. When was that? When? It seems like the first time now. But I've had it before, this feeling of exaltation: how can such a landscape exist, how *can* it be here, how can it *be* that there's . . . that there's . . .

1st KEEPER: That there's what?

JEAN: I'm amazed there can be such mountains, and the space, and this sky all round, resting on the peaks, then stretching out over the world.

1st KEEPER: It's perfectly natural. It's Nature.

JEAN: The long night is over.

1st KEEPER: Have you been asleep?

JEAN: No. Or rather, yes. Let's see now, what was I doing? Was I lying awake or drowsing? Anyway, I've woken to the wonder of the morning, of *this* morning at least. And I hope it's never going to end. I've been born again. That's what I came for, to make a fresh start. By that I mean, I'll be starting any time now. I'm a different person, yet I'm still the same one. I'd got too involved in things.

1st KEEPER: What things?

JEAN: Problems I thought were an essential part of myself. But *we* are not the things we do. That's why I can throw them off and find I'm still in one piece.

1st KEEPER: Well, that's all right then! Good . . . I'm glad, for your sake, to see you so happy. [*Enter the Second Keeper, who is very like the First.*] This gentleman's happy to be here. This gentleman is happy.

JEAN: Actually, I'm happy thinking how happy I'll be in a minute. Any moment now. She told me she'd be here. I'll have all I want in a minute. If I weren't so sure she'd be here, I'd have nothing at all. Hope, well-founded expectation, that's what makes me happy. There's still one tiny cloud in my sky, though it will soon blow away. Though I can almost feel her presence, behind that there's a void. But it's sure to be filled in the end. Bound to be. Nothing can stop her coming, we have a rendezvous. No-one made her promise. It was *she* who wanted it. I expect I'm a bit early. What time do you make it? [*To the First Keeper, who looks at his watch without saying a word. Jean looks at his:*] That's what *I* make it. [*To the Second Keeper:*] What time do *you* make it? [*The Second Keeper looks at his watch without saying a word:*] I'm right on time. [*To the First Keeper:*]

She will come, won't she? She can't help coming, can she?

1st KEEPER: You should know better than we do.

JEAN: We fixed a rendezvous. [*To the Second Keeper:*] We fixed a rendezvous. [*To the First Keeper:*] I've just arrived. A second here or there, what's the odds? Besides, we didn't decide on the second, or even the minute. A little leeway, that's natural. Can I go on waiting?

1st KEEPER: As long as you like, Sir. A good while, anyway. The museum's nowhere near closing-time yet.

2nd KEEPER: We have to stay here. It's our job.

JEAN: The curtain's lifted, the sky has cleared. Time for her to come! [*To the First Keeper:*] If the impossible happened and she didn't arrive today, could I leave word for her with you?

1st KEEPER: I don't know the lady.

JEAN: Don't ask me for her photograph. I must have had one, of course. What did I do with it? It can't be much good. I had a terrible camera. I could describe her to you. Perhaps she's been here before? Perhaps she waited for me and went away again? [*To the Second Keeper:*] You haven't seen a lady who looked as if she was waiting? You'd never forget her face. Perhaps she's been already? In which case, she's bound to come back. She didn't say anything to you?

1st KEEPER: I can't know all the folk, Sir, who visit the museum. I don't stare them all in the *face*.

JEAN: But I tell you *her* face is unforgettable! You couldn't help noticing *her!*

2nd KEEPER *to the First Keeper*]: Tell the gentleman that for a small consideration we'll keep our eyes open. If we remember this lady, if she's really been before, we'll tell him if she comes back. If it's her first visit, and it seems more likely to me, we'll have a closer look.

1st KEEPER *to Jean*]: Give us some means of identification, Sir, if you've no photograph on you.

JEAN: Identification?

1st KEEPER: Or tell us her name. We'll write it up at the entrance and then we could give her a message.

JEAN: I've forgotten her name.

1st KEEPER *to the Second Keeper*]: He's forgotten her name.

2nd KEEPER: Let him describe her, then.

JEAN: Describe her! Well, now! She's, she's, how can I say? Like a chapel on top of a hill. No, a temple suddenly emerging from the jungle. No, what she's really like is a hill, a valley, a forest, a clearing.

1st KEEPER: Please be more precise.

JEAN: She used to wear bracelets.

1st KEEPER: In our country all the women wear bracelets.

JEAN: She sails proudly along like a swan. I know! . . . That's not enough to go by.

1st KEEPER Is she dark, or fair, or a redhead?

JEAN: She had a dress with trimmings . . . a blue dress . . .

2nd KEEPER: Her eyes . . . What's the colour of her eyes . . . ?

JEAN: Misty eyes . . . no, black . . . no, very bright . . . and penetrating . . . no, elusive . . . with a present, no, absent look, the colour of certain dreams, as gentle as the touch of a warm river in summer. You see? She's easy to recognise!

1st KEEPER: I think if you had a photo or knew her name, it would be more helpful to us.

JEAN: I promise you'll recognise her by her smile. No-one smiles like her. She's on the tall side, I think, and she has long arms. But you'll recognise her too by the look of wonder on her face at finding herself here . . . She'll close her eyes a minute because the light's too strong. She'll ask you if I've been here, if you've seen me, if anyone's waiting for her. But will she know her self as her? Know

41

my self as me?

1st KEEPER: You didn't note on your memo-pad the actual date and time?

JEAN: Where can that memo-pad be?

1st KEEPER: How can you forget a memo-pad!

2nd KEEPER *to the First Keeper*]: Is he quite *sure* he didn't fix the rendezvous somewhere else?

JEAN: I'm sure it was here.

2nd KEEPER: I wouldn't be too sure, with a memory like yours.

JEAN: The past is coming back. I seem to remember now. I explained how she'd have to climb some steps to get here. I can see us walking side by side in the sunshine . . . I can still see our two shadows. I'd made it quite clear that to reach this place, before the steps, before the main flight, there was a dusty road by the sea. And before that, olive trees, the white town, the desert . . .

1st KEEPER: That's it. Those are the right directions.

JEAN: She said: "I'll come for sure". She couldn't have made that promise lightly, could she? Then she said: "I'll come for sure, even if I lose my memory, it will still be me. If *you* forget, it will still be you, it will still be us, just the same but without our memories." How can you lose your memory? We arranged to meet again, some year or other, in June, at eleven o'clock. At three o'clock in the afternoon? The fifteenth? The thirteenth? The seventeenth? Or was it to be in July?

1st KEEPER: You've lost *your* memory anyway. So how can I possibly help you?

JEAN: I think we changed the date to another, only a few days apart. That's what's muddled me up, that's why my mind's so confused. Hers too, I suppose. What did we decide, in the end? Let's see: the thirteenth, eleventh,

42

fifteenth, seventeenth, thirteenth, eleventh, fifteenth, seventeenth . . . She said: "Just now we can't, we're being watched. We're prisoners, with too many obligations!" But later on she'd come with me, to a country where everything starts afresh. I told her about *this* country, but it would take a long time to get here. A country with no station or airport. To reach it she'd have to pass through mournful plains, gigantic cities, and a desert. And climb mountains too. "To reach it", she echoed, "I'll pass through deserts and gigantic cities. I'll climb mountains too. Nothing shall stop me. I'll leave everything behind, burn all my boats." She *knew* it would take a long time.

1st KEEPER: I'm sorry, Sir, but I'll *never* recognise her. As you've nothing better to do, why don't *you* wait for her! If she promised, I expect she'll come. Don't worry!

JEAN: My description must seem a bit far-fetched to you.

1st KEEPER: Are you sure you'll recognise her?

JEAN: It's just possible her face is a little more lined, but she'll always have the same expression. I'll recognise her by the way she's trying to recognise me: she'll come, she told me she would. A meeting like this, of such vital importance . . . she'd have sent a cable, or written to explain. I'm so aware of everything all round me, yet I feel so empty inside. Something must be missing. What else can it be but her? Lost memories will guide her. Working deep down like grains of wheat, secretly seeking the light. She did all she possibly could, to be sure she wouldn't forget. "When we meet again", she said, "I'll have time for no-one but you . . . just for you . . . for my little Jean . . ." How did she put it? I'll only have time for you? For you? Or for my little Jean? I can hear her voice, but I can't hear her words any more.

43

1st KEEPER: Perhaps she has forgotten?

2nd KEEPER: Perhaps, in the meantime, she's made other appointments?

JEAN: If she'd forgotten, I'd have forgotten too. She knows *I'm* bound to come. And she knows, if *she* doesn't, I shall be tramping the roads, quite homeless, century after century, because she is my home, my haven. She'll come all right. Why don't we quietly enjoy these splendid mountains while we wait? Who's that? There she is! No, it must have been a mirage. May I sit down on this bench? [*He sits down on the bench, then gets up.*] Perhaps something unexpected stopped her from getting away. What a state she'll be in! Yet she told me she'd manage it, she promised: "I'll get there somehow, I promise. For your sake I'll come!" It wasn't a hasty decision, you know, but it was a spontaneous one. Spontaneity is the expression of a profound emotional . . . There she is! [*He makes for the back of the stage.*] No. I'm wrong: only the shadow of a bird on the wing. But once she *did* say: "We'll keep that for next time". Really she did! Is that her?

1st KEEPER: It's a trick of the light.

JEAN: Is that her? I can hear the crunch of sand beneath her feet . . .

2nd KEEPER: It's the wind.

JEAN: Oh! Why must we cling so to other people! What hope is there in someone else? "You'll find no hope", she'd say, "*except* in someone else. I'll teach you what joy is, I'll give you a zest for living that you've never known before." To think I wasted all those years, lived through them without living! "You'll have your time over again, *I'll* give it back." Did she really say that or is it my imagination? "What have you done with your life?" she asked. It's been one long nightmare. I've slept it away. "I'll keep

44

you awake, I promise. One fine morning, you'll wake up a different person, and yet you'll be just the same. The same person and someone else at one and the same time. And we'll live happy ever after. I'll teach you what life is!" But why doesn't she? Isn't that her climbing the steps? Is it still only the wind? Is it just that shadow again? Just the play of light? What's the time?

1st KEEPER: Midday.

JEAN: What's the time?

2nd KEEPER: One o'clock.

JEAN: What's the time?

1st KEEPER: Late afternoon.

JEAN: The evening's still a long way off. Can you hear her? I can: "Come along, here I am! Where are you?"

1st KEEPER *to the Second Keeper*]: Can *you* hear anything?

JEAN: The sun hasn't moved. It's not late. Not nearly evening yet. Can you hear her? I can: "Come closer! I want to see you!"

2nd KEEPER *to the First Keeper*]: I can't hear a thing.

1st KEEPER *to Jean*]: My partner and I can hear no voice at all.

2nd KEEPER: Do you remember her last words?

JEAN: Remember, dear? *I* can: "I love you, sweetheart, love you to distraction. Poor darling, don't worry!" That's what she said when she left me. She turned and went, in her blue dress, the smile of love on her lips. Oh! if only it would leave me, that vision of parting grace! She could not tear her love from her heart, from her heart she could not tear it, never from her heart could such love be torn, never, never, never! Can you see her coming? Can you hear her? Is she here yet? "Don't worry!" she said.

1st KEEPER: We're going to close the museum soon, Sir. Come back tomorrow. It may be she's forgotten.

45

JEAN: I love you, sweetheart, love you to distraction. Anyone who can't forget bears the scar for ever. Haven't *I* often lied, often made promises I've not been able to keep? Will I carry this mortal wound inside through all eternity? Mortally wounded, for ever. [*He sits down on the bench.*]

1st KEEPER: It's nearly closing-time.

2nd KEEPER: Time's getting on.

1st KEEPER: The sun's going behind the clouds. It'll soon be evening.

2nd KEEPER: The season's nearly over.

1st KEEPER: It'll soon be the start of another one.

2nd KEEPER: And that one won't suit him.

1st KEEPER *to Jean*]: It's late, Sir.

JEAN: "What have you done with your life?" she asked. "You've wasted it. But I'll give you a chance to live it all over again." Oh! If only she'd come! I can't manage all by myself. Is she climbing the steps? Is that the way she walks? Is she still just a shadow of the shadow of herself? Is it just a leaf? Is it just the wind? Or is it just the quiver of a wish? Just the whisper of a tear down my face?

1st KEEPER: That's it. Just a sigh from her lips.

JEAN: Show up in some form or other! I want to see you! Give some sign of life, at least! [*He looks round on all sides.*] I've no other refuge but you. There's nowhere I can live now. Who would welcome me? Oh, my friends, my keepers, I was so comfortable in my discomfort! Listen: and I'll tell you. I wanted to escape old age, keep out of the rut. It's life I'm looking for! Joy I'm after! I've longed for fulfilment and all I find is torment. I had to chooseb etween peace and passion. I chose passion, fool that I was! Yet I was safe enough in my hide-out, firmly locked in gloom and nostalgia, remorse and anguish, fears and responsibilities, like so many walls all round me. The fear of death was

46

my truest shield. Now the walls have collapsed. And here I am, defenceless, exposed to the blazing inferno of life, and in the freezing grip of despair. I wanted life and life has hurled itself at me. It's crippling me, killing me. Why didn't I have the sense to welcome resignation? All my old scars have opened, my wounds are bleeding again. Thousands of knives are driving into my flesh.

1st KEEPER: Why can't he lose his memory, and take refuge in oblivion?

2nd KEEPER: It's his own fault. Serves him right. He wanted everything, the glutton! He should have gorged himself on nothing.

1st KEEPER: For *forty* years I've been a keeper here. *I'm* not always on the move. I lead a quiet life. My wife's moustache is almost as big as mine.

JEAN: If only I'd been a mangy dog, or a cat that's out of sorts, all good ladies and dear old souls would come flocking round to carry me off and tend my sores and pamper me with pity. But I'm afraid I'm only a man. You can't take pity on a man: a man in pain is ridiculous to mankind.

1st KEEPER: Did *he* take pity on others?

2nd KEEPER: Everyone's looking for pity. They all want it for themselves. But no-one gives it to anyone else.

JEAN: Why did she drag me away from my slum, out of my tomb?

1st KEEPER: Wasn't he the one who said it's silly to suffer?

2nd KEEPER: Who advised indifference to others, or at the most a sneaking regard?

1st KEEPER: Who said you should idolise no-one? That not a living soul was deserving of veneration?

2nd KEEPER: Who claimed we should be free from the ties that bind us?

1st KEEPER: Who said nobody and nothing could ever belong to us?

2nd KEEPER: What a breach between heart and head!

1st KEEPER: What a contradiction!

2nd KEEPER: He doesn't believe what he thinks or think what he believes.

JEAN: What a breach between thought and life! Between myself and me! [*A woman seems to him to be passing over the terrace*:] Here she is! Is it really her? Is it you? Are you you? [*He has gone up to some invisible person.*] Isn't your name . . .? Let's see now, what is your name? . . . She's looking at me. She's going away. She *would* have recognised me! [*Another woman seems to him to be passing in the opposite direction.*] At last! . . . [*He rushes towards the shadow.*] I knew you'd come, after all the time I've been waiting! Since the beginning of time! Since the first time I was born.

1st KEEPER *taking on the voice of a woman*]: I don't know what you're talking about.

JEAN: Oh yes, you do! You know *me*! Open your eyes and have a good look! Gaze into mine. Don't you remember? Even if you don't, it's you all right. And I'm Jean. You've come for me, you were waiting for me.

2nd KEEPER *woman's voice*]: What impertinence! It's my husband I'm waiting for. And what's more, here he is!

1st KEEPER: It's late, Sir.

JEAN: Just a minute.

2nd KEEPER: What do you hope to obtain in one minute? Statistically, the laws of chance are against you. When it's centuries you've been waiting.

JEAN: And all that time I've been waiting for *her*, waiting for *you*.

1st KEEPER: The day is passing. It's gone.

48

2nd KEEPER: The week has gone.

1st KEEPER: The season has gone. We're off on our holidays.

JEAN: This life has gone. Once again, I'm afraid it's too late!

2nd KEEPER: Hope for another, you'll do better next time.

1st KEEPER: You'll find her.

2nd KEEPER: Or find her *again*.

1st KEEPER: Or you'll find another one . . . just like her.

JEAN: I don't want one of those women who all look alike and look like *her*.

1st KEEPER: You're fussy.

JEAN: I want the one all the others look like, not one who looks like her . . .

2nd KEEPER: We're just closing, Sir.

JEAN: The light is going. I admit it's getting late.

2nd KEEPER: We're closing, Sir.

JEAN: It's very late. It's too late. It's cold. The landscape's not the same any more. When hope fades, everything changes. [*He looks all round him.*] These are the gloomy plains of nightmare reality. The deserted plains and the marshes . . . What if that was all there was! My heart's like a wounded beast, clawing me in its death-throes . . . My stomach's a bottomless pit, my mouth a funnel of fire. Hunger and thirst, hunger and thirst . . . [*He goes now towards one keeper, now towards the other, or holds them both by the hand or the waist*:] You're my friends, my dear sweet Sisters! If only I could find that hide-out again where I dragged out my life, so cosy and snug, walled in by my fear of death . . .

1st KEEPER: And comfortable in discomfort. You told us that before. You should have stayed at home.

2nd KEEPER: You should have done what we did . . . the same as everyone else.

JEAN: Why did she uproot me? Why did she promise? I

49

didn't ask her to promise anything, did I?

1st KEEPER: She made you reflect the illusory light of love.

2nd KEEPER: There's no reason for living . . .

JEAN: Oh yes, sweethearts, pretend to pity me! [*The Keepers take out large handkerchiefs, wiping their eyes and blowing their noses.*] Thank you. It's a great help! I know there's no reason for living. I knew all the reasons for *not* living, for *not* plunging into life. I was cautious, my dears. If you knew how cautious I was, how suspicious . . . What memories did she stir in me, what nostalgia for the past, what secret wishes, what forgotten need? She awoke me to myself, she is absolute necessity. And I thought I could do without everying! Of course, of course, there's no reason for living. I found a *non*-reason . . . I clung to it and my hands got bruised . . .

1st KEEPER: That's what comes of being so unreasonable.

JEAN: Oh dear, oh dear, oh dear! Madness only pays if it means *total* darkness, if the mind is quite unhinged.

2nd KEEPER: You like the good life. Go and console yourself! We haven't had our dinner yet.

JEAN: To live like a living wound. I'm going, I'm going. I've been gone a long time, out on the roads to conquer the world. Plenty of roads, but not much world. Where shall I go? Where? Where can I find earth that's not hard, water that won't scald me, a dressing that heals, a bush without thorns? I am sick, my sweet ones. And I'm going away, far away. I'm dead. Yet I'm still dying. One word could cure me. But who is there that knows it? Who can utter it? I've forgotten where my old home is, I can't find the way. I'll go wandering on through the valley. Perhaps I'll meet her by chance. And yet they promised her to me, she was promised. I don't seem to understand. I'm going away. I'll go on so long as there's night, so long as there's day, so long as there's still twilight. [*Shouting*:] Where are you? I won't stop till I see the flashing of your crown.

1st KEEPER: Good luck on the road! It's a wide wide world. You're still young, you've plenty of time. *We* can't do any more.

2nd KEEPER: We've no desire. We're satisfied with little.

1st KEEPER *to Jean, who is disappearing towards the back of the stage*]: Come back and see us one of these days!

JEAN *you can hear him shouting*]: Appear and lighten my darkness! I need you because you're so alive, so dazzling, so gentle, intense and passionate and reassuring. [*His voice slowly fades.*]

2nd KEEPER: Who on earth *is* this girl? A sort of princess?

1st KEEPER: Do you think she exists?

2nd KEEPER: Aren't you hungry? Hm . . . I sniff the aroma of soup.

1st KEEPER: I can taste the wine in my mouth already.

2nd KEEPER: *Bon appétit!*

1st KEEPER: *Bon appétit!*

CURTAIN

III

THE BLACK MASSES OF THE GOOD INN

THE SET

The stage represents the main hall or refectory of a kind of monastery-cum-barracks-cum-prison. At the back of the stage you can see a large gate made up of quite widely-spaced bars. Behind these bars for the moment you can see a dismal landscape, indistinct, rather misty or overcast, empty. Later, right at the end, this landscape will be lit with a brilliant light, a great deal of green, trees and flowers, a very blue sky, at the final apparition of Marthe and Marie-Madeleine with a luminous ladder hanging down, exactly as in the final moment of the departure scene of the first act: "The Flight". Marthe, fifteen to sixteen, is the child from the cradle, now grown into an adolescent. This bright, Eden-like garden will contrast with the grey walls of the refectory.

In the refectory for the moment you can see, in the foreground, on the audience's right, a hearth without a fire. On the left a heavy old door, more or less Gothic, which creaks a little as it opens. Standing motionless in the middle of the stage is Brother Tarabas, who looks like a monk without looking quite like a monk, a hood over his head, but no cross. He remains like this for a few seconds. Then Brother Tarabas turns with a sharp movement towards the door and takes off his hood.

You can see Jean moving through the landscape, behind the iron gate, from one side to the other, and disappear for a brief moment. Knocking is heard.

TARABAS: Come in and welcome, guest. Come in. [*The door opens slowly, slightly creaking. Jean enters timidly, the door closes again. Jean is in crumpled clothes, he is ill-shaven and looks exhausted, older.*]

JEAN: Would you mind if I stopped here for a while? I can't go any further. I'm tired out. I've been walking for days, and I suddenly saw your place. May I have a little rest? I won't stay long. Don't worry, I don't want to be a nuisance. I'll soon have to be on my way again. I've seen so many things already and had all sorts of adventures. Very interesting, but quite exhausting. And my journey's not over yet. I just need a little rest before I carry on.

TARABAS: Make yourself at home. Take that stool and sit down. You can tell us all about it. [*Jean sinks down on the stool.*] That's the way, that's right.

JEAN *he wipes the sweat from his brow with a handkerchief, which he puts back in his pocket*]: It's very kind of you to let me stay.

TARABAS: We like to make visitors welcome here.

JEAN: Is this a monastery?

TARABAS: Not exactly. And yet, if you like, it is a *kind* of monastery. We never leave it. When people like yourself, who have travelled a great deal, come to pay us a visit, we're quite anxious for them to stay. We like to have some idea what's going on in the world.

JEAN: I'm really most grateful. Thank you.

TARABAS: *We* thank *you* for spending some time with us.

JEAN: No, I'm the one who . . .

TARABAS: No, we're the ones! [*Pause.*]

JEAN: Are you the Superior in this establishment?

TARABAS: By no means. I am Brother Tarabas. My task is to welcome strangers. [*Jean looks all round the room.*] You see, it's not exactly a monastery, is it? Nor is this room the guardroom of a barracks, as you might think. We're not a hospital either. In the course of centuries these buildings may have been used as a prison or a college, a monastery, a castle or a hotel. They're very old. They must have been used in many different ways. But things have changed now. This is an establishment, as you said. That's the very word, an establishment. We wear these habits for convenience. If we look like a religious order, that's because, in a certain way, religious we all of us are. No. I am not the Brother Superior. The Brother Superior is here with us now . . . [*The Brother Superior appears, abnormally tall, dressed in white; he could be raised up on stilts hidden beneath his homespun habit; the Brother Superior has come in on the audience's right. Jean stands up.*]

JEAN: My respects, Brother Superior.

TARABAS *to Jean*]: Please sit down. Our Brother Superior is a very simple man. [*To the Brother Superior, indicating Jean:*] This is our latest visitor. [*Then, after looking at the Brother Superior for a few moments, to Jean:*] The Brother Superior was expecting you, Monsieur. He bids you welcome, and thanks you for entrusting yourself to our care.

JEAN: Please thank him. I really mean it.

TARABAS: The Brother Superior is specially anxious for you to feel quite at home. So please sit down quietly and relax.

JEAN *sitting down again*]: You knew I was going to come?

TARABAS: We thought you would, we were almost sure. This is where people usually come. And you're here. That proves it.

JEAN *idiotically*]: That's true, yes, that's true. [*While Jean is making the speeches that follow, a second brother, then a third and a fourth, will come on discreetly, one after the other; the fourth one will sit down near the door, on the audience's left; the others will stand near Jean, when they have waited on him; the rest will*

54

sit on the ground, cross-legged in Eastern fashion.] It was very cold on the road. Then very hot. After that, very cold again. I feel rather cold even now. Is there a fire?

TARABAS: If you'd like one . . . The walls are very thick, that explains why it's so cool.

JEAN: And yet I'm thirsty.

TARABAS: Why not have a basin of hot water to soak your feet in? That will warm you up.

JEAN: Oh no! Really!

TARABAS: Why not? Yes! Take your shoes off . . . Your feet must have swollen . . .

JEAN: If you insist . . . [*Jean takes off his shoes. Tarabas goes towards the right, behind the small stretch of wall—in which a kind of porthole will appear at the end of the act—which juts forward slightly at the side of the stage; he will come back with a basin of hot water, and a towel, after the second brother has entered and brought Jean a jug.*]

JEAN *drinking out of the jug*]: Thank you, I was very thirsty. What was that? Water? Or wine?

TARABAS *to Jean, who is trying to dip his feet in the water while he drinks*]: Don't worry, let me do it! I'll wash your feet myself, you have a little drink.

JEAN *to Tarabas*]: All the same, I . . .

TARABAS: Don't be shy, it's the custom.

JEAN: I just drank it straight off, without thinking. I don't even know what I drank. Anyway, it was very good. Now I see: you keep a sort of inn in the old style, a rest-house for travellers.

TARABAS: A rest-house for travellers. Yes, that's it, if you like, the very word. You could call this place a sort of inn. Didn't you see the sign outside?

JEAN: I expect you're waiting for me to tell you about my journey: [*The third brother enters from the right bearing a tray*

55

on which there is a bowl and some bread.] Yes, please! I'm very hungry too. Thank you again.

TARABAS *at Jean's knees*]: Don't move. *I'll* dry your feet. Don't waste time, eat.

3rd BROTHER: Travelling always tires you and makes you hungry. It's only natural. You really need some refreshment. [*Enter a fourth brother who takes up his position, seated, near the door, on the audience's left. He is holding a carbine.*] That's our hunting brother.

JEAN: Oh yes! Yes! Yes! Yes!

TARABAS: We do our own hunting, we do our own fishing, we're market-gardeners and we make our own wine. Organisation's essential.

JEAN: It's extraordinary! [*He has his mouth full and swallows greedily.*] I eat and drink, eat and drink. And still I'm thirsty, still I'm hungry. I'm sorry, I must seem like a bottomless pit. In my whole life I've never been so hungry. It's true I've had nothing to eat for weeks, for months you might say. But you know, I hadn't even realised, I was so engrossed in my adventures, in the beauty and the marvels of the countries I went through.

TARABAS: You're lucky to have the chance to travel . . .

JEAN: That's true. Yes, I am lucky. I almost forgot about food and drink. May I have some more?

TARABAS: Take as much as you like, of course. We're at your service. [*To the second and third brothers*:] Help him to more, brothers, whatever he wants, as much as he wants. Don't let his bowl or his platter stand empty. Hurry, what are you up to? You must look after our guest. [*The second and third brothers bring Jean food and drink.*]

JEAN: Don't scold them, Brother Tarabas! It's my fault, I'm gobbling it down. They just can't keep up with me. [*Tarabas goes out with the basin and comes back with fresh towels, while Jean eats and drinks greedily, wildly; the brothers are constantly rushing in, rather comically, to replenish the dishes and go on serving Jean. Rhythmical movements.*]

TARABAS *to Jean*]: You must forgive them. They're slow, not so young as they were. A warm towel over your face makes you feel much better. [*Tarabas lays the towel over Jean's face. Jean removes it.*]

JEAN: Thank you. [*Between mouthfuls of food and drink*:] I must tell you my story too . . . I've so many things to say . . . I must tell you all about it.

TARABAS: No need to hurry. [*He again lays the warm towel over Jean's face.*]

JEAN *taking off the towel*]: It really does make me feel better . . . Oh! I've just thought! I don't know if I've enough money on me to pay for this magnificent meal.

TARABAS: Don't worry yourself about that! [*A further application of the towel between two mouthfuls of food and drink.*]

JEAN: I'd like to know . . .

TARABAS: It doesn't cost much.

JEAN: Still I . . . [*He takes off the towel.*]

TARABAS: Don't bother about it. We'll settle that later. We'll come to some friendly arrangement. Don't give it a thought.

JEAN *eating and drinking, very fast*]: You're so generous, so kind-hearted, friendship's a real vocation for you. It feels wonderful to be here!

TARABAS: Stay as long as you like.

JEAN: I wouldn't want to presume.

TARABAS: We're entirely at your disposal.

JEAN: It's so nice to be welcomed like this, it warms the cockles of the heart. But I'm afraid I must go in a minute. I've got to get back on the road. There's so much still to be seen, to be done, to be learnt!

TARABAS: Take a holiday, if you like . . . if you want to . . .

You're under no obligation . . . But we'd be delighted if you could devote a little time to us later on . . . as you suggested yourself . . . Just to talk, for a moment or two . . . and say a few words, over dessert, to our brothers and myself, to the Brother Superior, about the things you've seen. If you'd like to . . . Unless you're too pressed for time . . . There's no obligation . . .

JEAN: It's the least I can do.

TARABAS: Besides, your story's bound to be so absorbing it will be *our* turn to pay *you*. Are you still cold?

JEAN: I'm getting used to it, it's all right. No, no, it's not worth lighting the fire now.

TARABAS: Nothing pleases us more than entertaining visitors. Satisfy your hunger, quench your thirst. We'll have a small fire all the same. It's cosier. [*A monk lights the fire.*]

JEAN: No, no please, it's not worth it.

TARABAS *signing to Jean to drink*]: You must get warm and take proper refreshment. Don't be afraid, the bill can take care of itself. [*Jean goes on with his meal.*]

3rd BROTHER: Now, voyager! Tell us all the fine things you've seen!

TARABAS *to the 3rd Brother*]: Give him time to breathe.

2nd BROTHER *to Jean*]: How goes the world? Is it in a healthy condition?

TARABAS *to the 2nd Brother*]: Give him a chance to recuperate.

3rd BROTHER: Who have you seen then, voyager? What have you seen? [*The towel is applied again.*]

TARABAS: Wait! Wait a moment, can't you! [*To Jean:*] Our brothers are so impatient! Please forgive them! [*The towel is withdrawn.*]

JEAN: I understand perfectly. I feel better now, thanks to you. My tiredness has gone. If you don't mind, I'll eat a bit more of this in a moment, and drink some more of that.

3rd BROTHER: What have you seen?

2nd BROTHER: What have you heard?

[*The three brothers sit down in a circle round Jean. The fourth brother still remains motionless near the door. Brother Tarabas and the Brother Superior remain standing, Brother Tarabas closer to Jean. From time to time Tarabas casts a glance at the Brother Superior, as if asking his opinion, in a wordless exchange.*]

JEAN: *What* have I seen? What *have* I seen? Oh! So many things I can hardly remember. Everything gets mixed up. Wait . . . wait. I've seen people, and meadows, and houses, I've seen people, I've seen people, and meadows . . . Oh yes . . . Meadows and streams and railway-lines and trees . . .

3rd BROTHER: What trees?

JEAN: All kinds. Lots of them.

2nd BROTHER: Trees in blossom?

JEAN: Yes. Trees in blossom, trees that have lost their blossom, trees without blossom, trees without leaves and . . . Oh yes! Trees lining the roads. I've seen . . . children.

3rd BROTHER: What were the children doing?

JEAN: They were wearing satchels, on their way to school. On their way *from* school. Or else they were playing . . . at hopscotch or leap-frog or long tag. Lots and lots of children, dark and fair. Children . . .

2nd BROTHER: Did you speak to them? Did they say anything to you?

JEAN: Er . . . They were walking along. I overtook them on the road. There were others coming the other way. We passed each other and they just walked on. And then I saw other people, men and women. I couldn't talk to them all. I didn't speak to them. I hurried on. I hadn't got time. I wanted to arrive before it was dark. What am I saying?

Sometimes I travelled through the night as well. Then it was daylight again.

TARABAS: What kind of day?

JEAN: Grey and dismal over the plain, as far as the eye could see.

2nd BROTHER: Before the plain, on your way through the meadows, you must have seen the knight of olden times asleep on his feet in his armour like a statue.

3rd BROTHER: Did you go as far as the Palace? And see the Emperor, or his Attendants?

JEAN *eating*]: I told you: a dismal empty plain . . .

3rd BROTHER: Before the plain?

JEAN: There was sand and beaches.

2nd BROTHER: Then you must have seen the crimson ocean, the blood-red lakes and the chinks in the blue vault of Heaven, the rape of the stars and those contraptions whirling round in the shimmering rainbow sky?

JEAN: I saw the countryside, men and women quarrelling, weddings, yes, and lots of brides and bridegrooms.

3rd BROTHER: In the woods and the meadows, before the plain and the beaches, did you see the luminous springs, the crystal wolves, the petrified hag and the airy temples in space? [*Jean shakes his head.*] Temples with pillars reaching down to Earth?

JEAN: I've seen pillars of wood, pillars of church and state, yes, pillars of the pub, and pillars of hearth and home, I've seen pillar after pillar and people peregrinating . . .

TARABAS: We've plenty of pillars and peregrinating feet. How else could the universe go on, how could mankind progress?

JEAN: They'd stand up and go away, then they'd sit down, then they'd stand up again. Later on I saw some who were fast asleep, and then they'd wake up, they'd talk and

60

then they'd fall silent, speak no more, lie down to rest and never move again. They'd never be seen again.

3rd BROTHER: Did you see those lands that change colour as soon as you set foot there, with whole cities that are metamorphosed and towns like chameleons?

JEAN: I didn't see all that . . . I saw landscapes and towns and moustaches and mountains. What else do you want me to tell you? Moustaches and rivers and belts, turkeys and oranges, cannons and trucks, drunkards and white men and yellow and black, red houses, green houses, curtains and rivers and drums . . . I'm still hungry.

TARABAS: Don't be polite! Eat and drink! It's all yours for the asking.

JEAN: May I? Oh thank you, thanks. I'm eating and it's just as if I wasn't. A bottomless pit!

TARABAS: Our Brother Superior, if I interpret the expression on his face correctly, has not yet had his fill of the news you're giving us, which only increases *our* hunger and thirst.

2nd BROTHER: There's nothing new in what he's told us so far.

3rd BROTHER *to Tarabas*]: Ask him for something more exciting. Some memories are very well entrenched. Make him dig them out.

JEAN: The lowering plain, lonely paths, empty crossroads, wastelands.

TARABAS *to Jean*]: Tell us more. Before the deserted plain, before. You must have seen lots of other things. You're no ordinary traveller, you're an explorer. With sharper vision, longer memory, imagination.

JEAN *eating*]: I saw [*in between mouthfuls of food and drink*:] river . . . curtain, drum . . .

TARABAS *to Jean*]: Our Brother Superior will ask us to assess the value of this test. We must take notes. [*To the 3rd*

Brother:] Brother Accountant, Brother Psychologist, take note, take note. [*To Jean*]: Pull yourself together. Come on. Force yourself a little. We'll take it all into account.

JEAN *eating and loosening his collar and tie*]: Colour, river, drum, curtain, garden, belt, moustache. [*During this time the 3rd brother, the brother accountant, takes notes.*] Turkey, curtain . . .

3rd BROTHER: You've said that before.

JEAN: I'm choking . . . Let's see: cascade, drum, school, relative, house, sun, turkey, peasant, colour, garden, belt.

3rd BROTHER: You're repeating yourself, Brother Jean.

TARABAS *to Jean*]: You're repeating yourself, my dear sir. The Brother Superior isn't very impressed.

JEAN: I saw . . . I saw . . . garden, turkey, school, relative, sun, garden, garden.

3rd BROTHER: Not only is he repeating himself, but he's forgetting things. He's losing names and faces and objects on the way . . . He's losing everything on the way. What's more, he's not saying the words in the same order. [*To Jean*:] You're forgetting things, Brother Jean.

JEAN: No, I'm not, you know. [*He is trying to remember*:] River, curtain, turkey, drum. It's true, I'm remembering less and less . . . Ah . . . I've got it: peasant. Oh! And this is the word I'd forgotten . . . solstice!

3rd BROTHER *to Tarabas*]: That word doesn't exist in the vocabulary test we set him. [*To the 2nd Brother*:] He's inventing new words, so we don't notice the ones he's forgetting.

TARABAS *to Jean*]: You can't cheat, you know! This test's made up in such a way you can't fool anyone. None of us, or even yourself. But if you *are* inventing, other experiences, other memories, tell us about them.

JEAN: Belt, colour, colour, mask, mask, mask . . . The more I eat, the hungrier I get. The more I drink, the thirstier I get. My feet are cold.

TARABAS: Don't put your shoes on again. [*To the 2nd Brother*:] Put some sandals on him. [*To Jean*:] They'll keep you warm.

3rd BROTHER *to Tarabas*]: There are some words he always forgets. He never says them at all.

JEAN: I've noticed lately there are gaps in my memory. It's fatigue.

3rd BROTHER: You're overtired, that's true.

TARABAS: We'll get you back on form. This establishment of ours was once a clinic. We've a stock of medicine built up over the centuries by countless generations. It's all right, Brother Jean, these medicaments are imperishable.

2nd BROTHER: Imperishable. And fully tested.

TARABAS *pointing to the 2nd Brother*]: You can trust him, he's the brother who runs the pharmacy. We'll give you some pills you can take with you on the road. They'll improve your vision, so you'll remember what you've seen. You're so unobservant it's pathological. With renewed powers of concentration these sights and sounds will stick in your conscious mind. You'll have a more vivid imagination.

JEAN: And my fatigue? Yes . . . My fatigability.

TARABAS *to the 2nd Brother*]: His fatigability?

2nd BROTHER *to Jean*]: That will disappear. All you have to do, as you walk along, is to crunch these sweets.

3rd BROTHER: I've made a note of his answers to the test. It's only fair, if that. Slightly below the average.

TARABAS: Well now! We were hoping for something better. He couldn't even see the knight in armour. What's more, he doesn't remember the word.

3rd BROTHER: Not one allusion to the word.

JEAN: Did I know the word? I believe it was . . . No . . . I've forgotten . . . I'm sorry . . . But in self-defence I must say I went through some very thick fog. I could hardly make out the road, even a couple of yards in front of me.

TARABAS: The gold of the knight's armour shines through fog.

3rd BROTHER: He didn't see the exploding star. Or that luminous contraption plunging through the dark.

TARABAS *to Jean, indicating the 2nd Brother*]: Before you leave, he'll give you a secret remedy, put some visionary drops in your eyes.

3rd BROTHER: His hearing isn't up to much either, or else he'd have heard the explosion, or at least imagined it . . . [*A gesture from the Brother Superior. Tarabas turns towards him.*] . . . used his intuition.

TARABAS *to the Brother Superior*]: All right, Brother Superior. We'll ask him the questions in the second test. [*To Jean:*] You're a much-travelled man, we should very much like to know what has become of the friends who left us and went astray. These friends of ours must be needing help. They're probably short of food. Did you meet any beggars, with outstretched hands, along the road?

JEAN: I tell you I was making straight for my destination, staring ahead of me, walking fast.

TARABAS: Well, tell us about the towns, then.

JEAN: It was darkest night.

2nd BROTHER *to the 3rd*]: That's how it is when a soul is in distress.

JEAN: Sometimes it would be lighter. There, you see? You notice, I can remember? Then, in the distance, before I reached the deserted plain, before the fog came down, making a half-light which is neither day nor night, far away, when I was still a long way off and before the fog thickened, I could see the glow of forges, blast furnaces ablaze.

TARABAS: Did you approach? Did you pass through these towns?

JEAN: I approached several of them. They melted away. Or else the gates were closing. It was too early or too late, forbidden to enter!

3rd BROTHER: Still no precise information. Nothing to add to our documentation, our statistics. So you haven't really seen anything very remarkable, nothing that made any special impression on you, that caught your imagination, in the fields, in the towns, on the roads? No interesting conversation with anyone?

JEAN: There was no-one, no-one at all. While it was still light, as I told you, I did catch sight of a few figures . . . trooping about . . . yes, troops of figures, and then nothing, no-one. The fog came down.

TARABAS: You're sure you didn't hear the cry of a man, even if you didn't see him, that man drowning in the pool near the road you were on?

JEAN: I saw and heard nothing. It certainly didn't happen as I was passing. It was just before, I expect, or after. I would have heard. Or perhaps I'd have seen some shape in the water. The fog came down.

TARABAS: I'm sorry to insist, but when the darkness gave way, when the fog cleared, what was there then?

JEAN: I told you. There'd been curtains and rivers before. I told you. Believe me, that's all there was: the lowering plain, grey, deserted plain, as far as the eye could see. What a long plain it was! Then, the fog came down.

3rd BROTHER: Troops on the march?

TARABAS: Our brothers know nothing about it, Monsieur. They're like children. They don't bother you, I hope?

JEAN: Not at all. Why, yes, soldiers at dawn in serried ranks. With a sort of satchel on their backs. Like school-boys.

65

3rd BROTHER: Did you follow them? Where were they going?

JEAN: Towards some kind of sun. They vanished before they got there, enveloped in smoke or mist.

TARABAS *to the two Brothers*]: Our guest is getting tired of your questions.

JEAN: Again, the plain, then a harsh light . . . and then the fog came down.

TARABAS: Nothing else to report?

JEAN: No, nothing else. Ah yes, several times on my way—I hardly took any notice—several times on my way, through the fog or the dark night, at the corner of some wood or at the far end of a road, thanks to a brief shaft of light, from a flash of lightning or one of the moon's rays, a ghastly figure would appear, a ragged old woman leaning on a stick. She would stand quite still, and look at me without speaking. Yes, at rare intervals I did just catch sight of her in the darkness, almost bent double. I was right not to take any notice, wasn't I? It was a figment of my imagination, a trick my mind was playing, an old face such as I've never seen before, old age itself. I haven't seen her since. In my memory . . . the fog came down.

2nd BROTHER: Did you have a rest now and then, to get your breath back?

JEAN: When I couldn't walk any further, I'd stop, sit down on a milestone and shut my eyes.

TARABAS *more eagerly*]: And *then* what did you see?

JEAN: As I had my eyes shut . . .

TARABAS: Inside, what did you see? . . . What visions haunted you?

JEAN: The same: a lowering plain, a grey, muddy, endless plain, or paths that led nowhere, paths that led nowhere at all. And then the fog came down . . .

TARABAS: You're exaggerating. You don't seem to realise.

66

One of those paths must have led you to us.

JEAN: That's true. And I'm delighted. It was lucky for me you were here. I'm very grateful. How much do I owe you?

TARABAS *to Jean, after looking at the Brother Superior*]: Our Brother Superior wishes to thank you for giving us such a good talk about your travels.

JEAN: Oh well, you know! . . .

TARABAS: You're too modest, Monsieur Jean. It was more than a talk, it was a lecture, even if it was impromptu. It seemed thorough, carefully prepared, deceptively simple. I found it accurate and detailed, even if it lacked the usual touch of rhetoric. You're a genuine case, I'm quite sure of that. You probably noted our brothers were making notes. *They* were noting *you*. Nothing will be lost, not a single word you said. We're very grateful to you. Now we wish you to relax and enjoy yourself. What would you say to an amusing entertainment? Don't say no, we'd be most upset. Make yourself comfortable. You mustn't have any complaints when you leave. Please don't thank us. When you go out into the world again, a world we can never know, cloistered as we are, we'd like you to give our establishment a good recommendation. We want to ask you straightaway to forgive any deficiencies in the show we're going to put on. It's amusing, I hope, as I said. Instructive perhaps too. *Utile cum dulci.* Anyway, we do our best. Don't forget we're amateurs. Imagine we have among us two characters suffering from a traumatic education formation or, if I may say so, progressive malformation. Having become what they are, they have reached a point from which they must set off again and follow the other route. Each of these characters has to learn the contrary of what he knows. It's all in the artist's

67

imagination, of course. I see by the expression on your face that you don't understand me very well. It's a play about education and re-education. You'll see. [*The 3rd Brother looks at the Brother Superior, then:*]

3rd BROTHER *to the 2nd Brother, discreetly*]: I believe our Brother Superior agrees with me. The results of Monsieur Jean's tests are not good enough.

2nd BROTHER: They're unenlightening.

TARABAS *to the two Brothers*]: Be quiet. We're beginning.

[*Two iron gates like two cages descend from the flies: two characters quickly enter them and take off their monks' habit, while two Brothers close the gates of the cages. Or else the cages arrive from the wings, with Tripp and Brechtoll inside, pulled in on tracks, or pushed on some other way. The two prisoners are old. The two Brothers push on a trolley bearing a bowl, a cooking pot and a ladle. They each make for one of the cells.*]

TARABAS *to Jean*]: You already know the Brothers who play the jailors. I'm afraid they don't look fierce enough for the parts. The two seedy characters in the cages are the prisoners. They used to be professionals: real clowns. What we're about to show you might be called a didactic entertainment. It was produced by our Pedagogical Brother, who's in charge of our various education and re-education courses. [*He turns towards the Brother Superior:*] Brother Superior, my task is to welcome strangers, I cannot . . . It's not one of my functions . . . [*Silence from the Brother Superior.*] Very well, Brother Superior. [*To Jean:*] Our Brother Superior tells me our Pedagogical Brother has, at this moment, other fish to fry . . .

JEAN: Fish to fry?

TARABAS: So I'm obliged to take his place on the spur of the moment. It will be far from perfect. Still, I hope you'll be able to follow the action. Sit there, you'll see better, it's

68

the place of honour . . .

[*More Brothers arrive, representing the audience. Two of them are carrying an armchair and a platform on which they install Jean as if at the theatre. The others, more humble members of the audience, sit down on either side of Jean on chairs they have brought. They will look on fixedly, emotionless, at least at the start. When the play starts, they take off their hoods and reveal their lack-lustre faces. The monks on Brechtoll's side are dressed in red and flooded with red light; those on Tripp's side are dressed in black. Each group will, while the other remains still, show its appreciation at the critical moments, by rhythmical applause, by collective ryhthmical movements, and appropriate mime, of the words Tarabas addresses to one or the other of the prisoners. Jean will also mime his anguished participation in this dual reaction. He will reflect the passion of the two prisoners. His mime contrasts with the alternating attitude of approval and disapproval of the two camps in the audience; he thus expresses the anguish of both prisoners, he "participates", he identifies himself with both; from time to time, especially at the start, he seems idiotically not to understand, he is stupefied, he laughs even, thinking it a game; then his reactions become pained and dramatic as he gradually comes to understand and he turns to face the audience of monks, mutely questioning them.*]

Do sit down, then . . . No, please . . . Don't be shy . . .

JEAN: I don't want to look as though I'm presiding . . . This is the Brother Superior's seat . . .

TARABAS: Come along . . . No false modesty . . . Take your seat . . . Not another word . . . The play's about to begin . . .

[*During this dialogue, the other Brothers have settled down on their seats, the Brother Superior behind, impassive, dominating everyone by his height. Tarabas puts on a more sumptuous cloak, red on Tripp's side, black on Brechtoll's side; he throws a*

69

hood over his head, also red and black, with great holes for his eyes, leaving his lips free.] How are you, Mr. Tripp? How's the morale? Still in prison! I'm afraid it's not very exciting for you! But you must make the best of it. Your faith will help. You're not sulking, are you? That's not very nice. [*Turning towards the other prisoner:*] Dear Mr. Brechtoll!

TRIPP (*to Tarabas*): *while Tarabas is speaking to Brechtoll*]: Please, open this door and give me back my freedom.

TARABAS *to the public, in other words to Jean, the monks, and so to the audience too*]: They all say the same thing. Whether it's their fault, or someone else's, or nobody's fault at all, as soon as they land in prison, they want to get out again. They want their freedom. All freedom is provisional.

BRECHTOLL: I want my provisional freedom.

TARABAS *to Brechtoll*]: You see, Mr. Brechtoll, Mr. Tripp, next door, is also in prison, but for different reasons, for exactly the opposite ones. He'd like to get away too. As for me, there's nothing I'd like more, but I'm afraid you're not the only two prisoners! After all, I can't let everyone out. Just imagine! Thousands and thousands of people at liberty, dashing all over the place, roaming pell-mell through the streets? Think of it: the prisons empty and the streets packed with people wandering aimlessly about. It would turn the world inside out. I can't risk a traffic-jam like that. [*Laughter from Jean, the others do not laugh.*] Let me put myself in your place, Mr. Tripp, in my thoughts, of course. Let me put myself in your place, Mr. Brechtoll. I can see why you find it hard to understand me. After all, it's because you don't understand *yourselves* that you're both where you are now. What would you be free from? Catching your death of cold? [*Laughter.*] Here, you're protected from the cold. Being struck by lightning? Here,

70

on the roof, we have a lightning conductor. Here you're free from all attachments . . . Just now you're in one sense attached to this place, it's true, but our strongest attachments are emotional. Yes. You're in a real prison when your mind is alienated. Aren't you, Mr. Brechtoll? Physical torture, for example, frees you from moral torment. When we were torturing you, did you think about anything else? Free yourself from the idea of getting away: it will be a great relief to you for a start. Your conscious mind is full of lingering doubts, old habits that cling to you: systems, doctrines, dogmas, myths, ticks, automatic mental reactions that get in your way. Shake them off, these relics of a faulty education. Oh! How tenacious they are! Ready-made ideas are very stubborn. When you've cast off your pitiful prejudices, you'll be almost free or at least prepared for freedom. [*The next four speeches should run together almost simultaneously.*]

BRECHTOLL: We know that speech. It's the hundredth time you've made it.

TRIPP: You've not convinced me.

BRECHTOLL: All based on a theory with no foundation in fact.

TRIPP: Vague ideas.

TARABAS: Up to a point I admit your objections. You're right. Anything that's not verified by experience is purely theoretical, hazy in it's abstraction. The time has come to put it to the test. If you don't want to suffer, you needn't. You'll only suffer so long as you enjoy it: you can stop by yourselves whenever you want to. It's your happiness we're after, Gentlemen, *your happiness.* [*Rhythmical applause from both sides, Red and Black.*] We'll just put you on a course to disintoxicate you. You'll be purified, wiser than before. Your minds will grow more supple and you'll be completely free.

71

TRIPP: Then will we be allowed to go? [*Indignant movements from the Red Side.*]

BRECHTOLL: Will the cage be opened? [*Indignant movements from the Black Side.*]

TARABAS: What terminology! When you've been disintoxicated, you won't see things in the same way at all: what you now call your cage you'll know by its proper name. Your outlook will be different. Your intelligence cleansed. Your deep-rooted beliefs . . . Well, you'll see! Anyway, the three of us, you two and I, are going to proceed with the verification of what seem to you our hypothetical theories. In thirty lessons, released from all your obsessions, you'll be like these two enlightened brothers [*he indicates the Second and Third Brothers*] who are here just to be of service, just to help you. They've passed their apprenticeship in the art of un-learning already, they've been through the same stages as you. Are they complaining? Look at them, the very idea makes them laugh. It will all go perfectly. Thirty lessons, no more. Thirty. Today is the first. [*Miming from Jean. The others remain impassive.*]

2nd BROTHER *to Brechtoll*]: Are you hungry, Mr. Brechtoll? It's lunchtime. There's a succulent soup. It smells delicious!

[*simultaneously*]

3rd BROTHER *to Tripp*]: Are you hungry, Mr Tripp? There's a succulent soup. It smells delicious!

TRIPP: I don't want any of your soup, or your bread either.

BRECHTOLL *almost simultaneously*]: I'd rather starve to death. Open the door!

2nd BROTHER *to Brechtoll*]:   There's nothing shameful in feeling hungry.

[*simultaneously*]

3rd BROTHER *to Tripp*]: There's nothing shameful in feeling hungry.

TARABAS *to Brechtoll, then to Tripp*]: It's lunchtime. Risk it. Have some. [*Hesitation from Brechtoll and Tripp.*] If you *weren't* hungry, we'd be cross. We've taken a lot of trouble to prepare you some good soup. [*To Brechtoll:*] You're only a prisoner, of course. [*To Tripp:*] You're only a prisoner, of course. [*To them both:*] But we don't despise you for that. [*Jean mimes his relief.*] We didn't want to kill a man for the error of his ways. [*To Brechtoll:*] Subjectively speaking, you're not guilty. [*To Tripp:*] We are charitable men. [*The murmurs of approbation and indignation, the carefully measured and highly rhythmical applause of the audience, Red and Black, should be regulated by the director. To both:*] We want to set you on the way of truth. We wish for your salvation. For that we must keep you in good health. [*To Tripp:*] We care about your health, Mr. Tripp. [*To Brechtoll:*] We like you, Mr. Brechtoll. [*To both:*] Sincerely, from the bottom of our hearts.

3rd BROTHER *to Tripp*]: What a lovely smell!
    [*simultaneously*]
2nd BROTHER *to Brechtoll*]: What a lovely soup!

TARABAS *to both*]: If you don't eat, if you lose weight, if you fall ill, it's we who will be punished. You wouldn't want to get us into trouble! Come, Mr. Brechtoll, show willing! Mr. Tripp, show willing! [*A clock can be heard striking.*] Midday. Time for a meal. [*The two prisoners do not answer.*]

2nd and 3rd BROTHERS *together*]: It's time for a meal.

TARABAS *to the two Brothers*]: They'll feel hungry eventually. Keep the soup hot. [*To Brechtoll:*] The meal's ready. [*To Tripp:*] The meal's ready. [*The clock is heard striking.*]

3rd BROTHER *to Tripp*]: It's one o'clock. [*The clock is heard again.*]

2nd BROTHER *to Brechtoll*]: It's two o'clock. [*Clock.*]

3rd BROTHER *to Tripp*]: It's three o'clock. [*Clock.*]

2nd BROTHER *to Brechtoll*]: It's four o'clock. [*Clock.*]

JEAN *shouting desperately from his seat*]: Six o'clock, Mr. Tripp. [*Clock. All the Red Side turns towards Jean in brief astonishment.*]

2nd BROTHER *to Brechtoll*]: Nine o'clock, Mr. Brechtoll. [*Clock.*]

3rd BROTHER *to Tripp*]: Midnight, Mr. Tripp. [*Clock.*]

2nd BROTHER *to Brechtoll*]: Midnight, Mr. Brechtoll. [*Clock.*]

3rd BROTHER *to Tripp*]: Midday, Mr. Tripp.

JEAN *as before*]: Midday, Mr. Brechtoll. [*Clock, same reaction from the Black Side.*]

3rd BROTHER *to Tripp*]: Midday, Mr. Tripp.

2nd BROTHER *to Brechtoll*]: Midday, Mr. Brechtoll.

3rd BROTHER *to Tripp*]: Three o'clock. You're still not hungry, Mr. Tripp?

[*simultaneously*]

2nd BROTHER *to Brechtoll*]: Three o'clock. You're still not hungry, Mr. Brechtoll?

TARABAS *to both*]: Admit you are. It won't commit you in any way. Then we'll give you back your freedom.

TRIPP: You're mocking me. You're lying.

BRECHTOLL: You're lying.

TARABAS *looking first at one, then at the other*]: We respect you too much for that.

BRECHTOLL: I mistrust any kind of soup. [*Laughter from Jean. Disapproving murmurs from the Red and Black Sides. Jean is shocked into silence.*]

TARABAS *to both*]: You're making a mistake.

2nd and 3rd BROTHERS *together, while the clock can still be heard, rattling bowls and ladles*]: Four o'clock, five o'clock, six o'clock. Who's hungry? Who wants his nice sou-soup?

We're taking the soup away! [*They make as if to leave.*]

TARABAS *to the Brothers*]: Wait, be patient! *They* are patient enough, poor devils.

BRECHTOLL: I want a drink.

TRIPP: I'm thirsty, I'm hungry. [*Jean swallows as if he had a dry throat.*]

TARABAS *turning to the Brother Superior*]: They haven't held out more than a week. [*To the two prisoners:*] Congratulations! Congratulations! I've known others far more obstinate than you. I don't suppose you're used to prolonged fasting. It's better this way. You see, Mr. Tripp, you see, Mr. Brechtoll, how stupid it is to go on a hunger strike. Our prison soup is so good: our cooks are excellent. [*To Brechtoll:*] Now, you'll be served. [*To Tripp:*] Now, you'll really be served.

BRECHTOLL: Hurry up!
            [*together*]

TRIPP: Quickly! Let's get it over!

TARABAS *to first one, then the other*]: Straightaway, straightaway. [*To both:*] You'll get served, don't worry. However, the Brother Superior has noticed you're not observing protocol. He insists you respect the rules and have good manners.

BRECHTOLL: I want some food, Brother, please!
        [*together*]

TRIPP: My soup, Brother, please, my soup, my soup!

TARABAS: That's not the way. Don't clutch at those bars, it's forbidden. Don't poke your arms out through them like starving men. [*To the two Brothers:*] Step back a few feet, or they'll knock everything over. [*To Tripp and Brechtoll:*] If you upset the plate, there'll be no more soup. [*To Tripp:*] Why do you say "my" soup? It's "our"

75

soup. We prepared it with the vegetables from our kitchen-garden, with the water from our well drawn by our own Brothers. We even put some of our butter in it. Let it be clearly understood it is "our" soup. We don't mind sharing it with you, we don't mind at all, on certain conditions. [*To Brechtoll:*] On certain conditions. [*To Tripp:*] Certain conditions.

BRECHTOLL: Please, *please* have the goodness to give me some food!

TRIPP: For charity's sake, something to eat and drink!

TARABAS *to Brechtoll*]: What do you understand by goodness, Mr. Brechtoll? You appeal to my goodness. You believe in goodness. [*To both:*] You'll get your soup, all right, now I've said you will. Formalities first, though. We're not short of time or victuals. [*To the Second Brother:*] You'll give Mr. Brechtoll his food, pedagogically. [*To the Third Brother:*] And Mr. Tripp his, pedagogically. [*To the Second Brother:*] These gentlemen are human beings. We must not fling their food at them as if they were wild beasts. Methodically, Brothers.

JEAN *going towards Tarabas*]: Listen, Brother Tarabas!

TARABAS *turning towards Jean*]: I beg pardon?

JEAN: Do I have to sit through the whole scene? [*Murmurs from both sides, Red and Black.*]

TARABAS: As you wish. It would be unseemly to leave without seeing the rest. The actors would be annoyed. The Brother Superior is putting this show on for *you*. It won't last too long. We know you're in a hurry. Go and sit down. [*Jean goes back to his seat. To Brechtoll:*] If we gave you something to eat, would it be out of the goodness of our hearts? Wouldn't it be simply justice? [*To Tripp:*] You appealed to our charity, didn't you?

TRIPP: Yes.

TARABAS: You are charitable, Mr. Tripp. I understand that. But if we gave you something to eat out of charity, that would be humiliating. We should give you some food because you deserve it. [*To Brechtoll:*] This goodness, where does it come from? Do you believe that we are good, that we are just or unjust? [*To both:*] You must be cold in your cells. I'm sorry. The soup will warm you up. Would you like your soup first or your freedom? You're too weak to go straight across the plains to the foot of the mountains, and then climb them and pass the frontier that's right at the top. So soup first. We'll open the gates later. [*To Tripp:*] Do you deserve your soup?

TRIPP: I don't know. I'm hungry.

TARABAS *to Tripp*]: How does it come about that you don't know? [*To Tripp and Brechtoll:*] Try and restrain yourselves a moment. Have patience. [*To Brechtoll:*] The soup is good. In your opinion, are we as good as our soup, are we not so good, or are we good in a different way?

BRECHTOLL: I don't believe in your goodness, I don't believe the soup is good. But it's food.

TARABAS *to first one, then the other*]: So you do deserve your soup? So you do deserve your soup?

TRIPP: I've done nothing wrong, so I do deserve it. It's next to nothing.

TARABAS *to Brechtoll*]: So we're meant to be basically wicked?

BRECHTOLL: Man is neither good, nor wicked.

TARABAS *to Tripp*]: If you deserve it, why did you say "something to eat, for charity's sake" and not "because I've deserved it"?

BRECHTOLL: I've demystified goodness. I know what's behind it. Everything depends on the compromises we reach. [*The Red Side applauds—disapproval from the Black Side.*]

TARABAS *to Tripp*]: You said "Something to eat, for charity's sake". So you think us unjust, but you also think us charitable.

BRECHTOLL: Some agreements just spring from necessity.

TARABAS *to Brechtoll*]: What necessity? [*To Tripp*:] Why have we put you in there, Mr. Tripp?

TRIPP: I don't know.

TARABAS *to Tripp*]: Is it for our own pleasure?

TRIPP: I don't know.

TARABAS *to Tripp*]: By mistake?

TRIPP: I don't know.

TARABAS *to Tripp*]: Is it because we are wicked?

TRIPP: I don't know.

BRECHTOLL: I mean social necessity: we live in a community.

TARABAS *to Brechtoll*]: So we reach compromises, but there's no-one to see us?

BRECHTOLL: Who could see us?

3rd BROTHER *to Tripp*]: Are we meant to be guilty on your account?

TARABAS *to Brechtoll*]: So no-one can see us? No-one up there or down below?

BRECHTOLL: I don't know what you mean.

TRIPP *to Tarabas*]: I can't know whether you're good or wicked. We'll talk about that later. Give me my rations, you promised.

TARABAS *to Tripp*]: As you wish. Just tell us if you think we've wronged you, yes or no. [*To Brechtoll*:] If no-one's there to see us, or compels me to be good, who's to stop me starving you to death? If you annoy me, I can break the agreement.

TRIPP *to Tarabas*]: Yes. Yes. You have wronged me.

3rd BROTHER *to Tripp*]: So if we put you in a cage it is because we are wicked? Be more explicit if you want your pittance.

BRECHTOLL *to Tarabas*]: That's right. No-one compels you to keep the agreement. I'm in your power.

TARABAS *to Brechtoll*]: So I can starve you to death with impunity!

TRIPP *to Tarabas*]: No, it wasn't exactly because you're wicked you put me here. I can hardly stay on my feet. I'm hungry.

BRECHTOLL: Please stop playing this little game.

TARABAS *to Tripp*]: Hang on. If it's not through our wickedness, what *is* the reason? [*To Brechtoll*:] I wouldn't allow myself to play games. [*To Tripp*:] What *is* the reason? [*To Brechtoll*:] I understand: we're all meant to hate one another? Or at any rate feel indifferent. In that case, in whose name do you ask me not to starve you to death?

2nd BROTHER *to Brechtoll, rattling his ladle*]: No-one's responsible to anyone.

TRIPP: You promised, you promised.

TARABAS *turning towards Tripp*]: You're about to collapse . . . Ah! Now you're standing up straight again. No, don't faint. Doesn't it smell good! [*To the third Brother*:] Lift up the lid. The aroma alone will give him back his strength. [*To the second Brother*:] Lift the lid for Mr. Brechtoll too, we mustn't be unfair to him. The smell does me good as well and gives me an appetite. [*The Third Brother makes as if to offer the ladle to Tripp. He withdraws it, then offers and withdraws it again. The Other Brother does the same in front of Brechtoll's cage. From his seat Jean makes the gesture of offering a ladle. To Tripp*:] Now tell us, if you're not here for our pleasure, nor because we're wicked, what are you here for?

TRIPP: It's all a mistake.

TARABAS *to Tripp*]: Do you think we mistook you for someone else? We've got record cards on everyone. All kinds of photographs and files. We know what everyone has done, what everyone has thought, what everyone has ever thought or done. We have the finest filing experts. We cannot be mistaken.

TRIPP: That's not what I mean. You're not mistaking me for someone else. Your mistake is an error in your thinking. I'm hungry.

BRECHTOLL *to the Brother who is pushing the ladle under his nose and pulling it back again.*]: Stop that! Please!

TARABAS *to Brechtoll*]: Again?

2nd BROTHER *to Brechtoll*]: In the name of what, in whose name?

JEAN *from his seat*]: In the name of what, in whose name?

BRECHTOLL: In the name of nothing.

TARABAS *to Tripp*]: An error of judgment? There was no trial. [*To Brechtoll:*] Do you believe in nothing, Mr. Brechtoll?

3rd BROTHER *to the public*]: A trial is just ritual. Judgement precedes the trial.

TARABAS *to Tripp*]: So we're meant to have made an error in our reasoning? Now, is that likely? [*To Brechtoll:*] I'm sorry, but you don't believe in God?

BRECHTOLL: What's God got to do with all this?

TRIPP: I'm hungry.

TARABAS *to Tripp*]: I know, I know. But answer. I'm hungry too, and thirsty, for your words. [*To Brechtoll:*] Speak without concealment. I wish to know your deepest thoughts, and then you'll have your soup. [*To Tripp:*] Speak your mind, answer. [*To Brechtoll:*] Don't mince your words.

TRIPP: In the state I'm in . . .

3rd BROTHER *to Tripp*]: You wouldn't be in this state if you hadn't refused the meal we tried to serve you. Obstinacy is a bad thing. It gets you nowhere.

TARABAS *to Brechtoll*]: Yes or no, do you believe in God? [*To Tripp*:] Make yourself clear: in your opinion, has this mistake affected your particular case?

TRIPP: That's not the right approach.

BRECHTOLL: No, I don't believe in God. How could anyone believe in Him? [*Various reactions on the Black Side.*]

TRIPP *to Tarabas*]: There's no fault in your reasoning. That you should arrest me is perfectly logical, in accordance with your scale of values. It's just that, with you, there's a fundamental error, which all your doctrine's based on.

TARABAS *to Brechtoll*]: You unhappy man, not to believe in God! [*Pointing his finger at Brechtoll, vehemently:*] That's why you imagine all mankind is wicked. That's why you invent this unlikely solidarity between men. [*To Tripp:*] We have no doctrine. But you have prejudices. [*To Brechtoll:*] This human solidarity you speak of, what else could bind men together, but God?

BRECHTOLL: We have no basic principles. Necessity binds them together. We'll discuss it after the meal, after the meal, after the meal.

TRIPP *to Tarabas*]: On what do you found your scale of values then?

TARABAS: What scale of values?

TRIPP: Whatever induced you to put me in prison, for example.

TARABAS *shrugging his shoulders, smiling*]: Such questions are beyond me. I had my orders.

BRECHTOLL: I answered: No. I gave you a definite No. So give me something to eat as you said you would if I gave a straight answer yes or no.

TARABAS *to Tripp*]: Mr. Tripp . . .

BRECHTOLL *to Tarabas*]: Now I've answered No, keep your word.

TRIPP: For charity's sake, Sir . . .

3rd BROTHER *to Tripp*]: Call me "Brother".

TRIPP *to Tarabas*]: For charity's sake, Brother . . .

TARABAS *to Brechtoll*]: Keep my word? By virtue of what agreement? You're of no use to me. [*To Tripp:*] We have no doctrine . . .

BRECHTOLL: I can't go on standing any longer.

TARABAS *to Tripp*]: . . . no principles, no values: we are free.

2nd BROTHER *to Brechtoll*]: Still hungry?

TARABAS *to Tripp*]: If you've been imprisoned, it's because *you* have belief, values, a doctrine—[*turning his head towards the Second Brother:*] what does he call it?—a moral system. [*To Tripp:*] In other words, prejudice. You are not *our* prisoner. It is your *thought* that imprisons *you*.

2nd BROTHER *to Brechtoll*]: I don't know whether I should serve you or not. How does it serve us to serve you?

BRECHTOLL *to the 2nd Brother*]: I'm not asking you for anything else.

TRIPP: Freedom, that's my choice.

2nd BROTHER *to Brechtoll*]: You'd rather starve to death?

BRECHTOLL: I'd rather.

TARABAS *to Tripp*]: A philosopher, even when he's half starved! You're going to starve to death, poor Mr. Tripp. And I was just thinking of giving you back your freedom. [*To Brechtoll:*] You'd rather starve to death. And I was just thinking of helping you to regain your freedom . . . You see, you're not indifferent to everything.

3rd BROTHER *to Tripp, brandishing his ladle*]: Eat first? Or get away first?

TARABAS *to Brechtoll*]: You believe in neither good nor wickedness, you don't believe in God. You believe in soup and freedom. And yet this thing which is so precious to you and which you cannot define is what I wanted to give

82

you back: your freedom.

TRIPP: Let me eat first. Then you can open the door of the cage. Right now, I'm too weak.

TARABAS *to Tripp*]: You've made your choice: to eat first. Which means: to stay where you are. Now you can see that choice imprisons.

BRECHTOLL: You're lying.

TARABAS *to Brechtoll*]: You abuse me, but I forgive you.

BRECHTOLL: Let me get out.

TARABAS *to Brechtoll*]: We'll do as you say. [*To Tripp:*] We'll do as you say. [*To them both:*] It's agreed. We'll give you something to eat first and open the door for you later.

BRECHTOLL: Open it.

TARABAS *to Brechtoll*]: I've told you before, you'd collapse on the road.

TRIPP: Just a bowl of steaming soup for now, that's all, for charity's sake.

TARABAS *to Brechtoll*]: First, build up your strength! [*To Tripp:*] Really, it's an obsession! You've always got the word charity on your lips. Will that feed you? No, it won't, will it?

BRECHTOLL: Will you let me out after the meal?

TARABAS *to Brechtoll*]: To go and imprison yourself somewhere else? But that doesn't matter, it's your own affair.

TRIPP *to Tarabas*]: For the love of God.

TARABAS *to Tripp*]: So you *do* believe in God, Mr. Tripp? [*To Brechtoll:*] Yes, you can go if you eat. [*To Tripp:*] The love of God isn't a linguistic obsession, definitely not. Do you believe in God. Answer! No need to be shy about believing in God. Come along, yes or no? It's not difficult to answer. Yes or no, do you believe in God? [*To Brechtoll:*] Know that nothing binds me to give you your ration. No promise, even your word, nothing. Unless, perhaps, you pray.

TRIPP *to Tarabas*]: I believe in God, yes, I believe.

TARABAS *to Tripp*]: That question was simply a formality. We know you believe in God, in divine mercy.

BRECHTOLL: I have prayed you, yes, and I'm praying you now.

JEAN *from his seat*]: He's praying you now.

TARABAS *to Brechtoll*]: You must *pray*, not just pray *me*.

TRIPP *to Tarabas*]: Yes, I believe in His mercy and His charity.

TARABAS *to Brechtoll*]: And it is not to me you should address this prayer.

BRECHTOLL: To whom? To the Brother Superior?

2nd BROTHER *to Brechtoll*]: To Someone even more highly placed.

TARABAS *to Tripp*]: All this chatter won't assuage your hunger.

BRECHTOLL *to the 2nd Brother*]: Is there someone more important in this institution?

TARABAS *to Tripp*]: Let's break off this discussion: You're famished.

BRECHTOLL: Is it allowed to make a request in writing?

TARABAS *to Tripp*]: As God can do anything, you have the solution, pray *Him* to give you something to eat. His soup is better than ours.

TRIPP: But . . .

3rd BROTHER *to Tripp, making as if to go away*]: His soup is better than ours.

BRECHTOLL: Some paper and I'll sign it.

TARABAS *to Brechtoll*]: There is One who is above all institutions. He is not written to. He is spoken to, invoked. He alone can give orders. We listen to none but Him.

TRIPP *to the 3rd Brother*]: I'm praying you.

JEAN *from his seat*]: He's praying you.

TARABAS *to Brechtoll*]: Don't pray *me*, my friend. Pray to the

84

Almighty Lord.

BRECHTOLL: So there's nobody, then.

TARABAS *to Tripp*]: Come along. Say "Our Father which art in Heaven". You don't know that prayer? [*To Brechtoll*:] Only to Him of whom I speak can you address yourself. How obstinate you are! What blindness! Your freedom is at hand and you don't want it.

TRIPP: "Our Father which art in Heaven, blessed be thy Name."

BRECHTOLL: But I *do* want my freedom.

TARABAS *to Tripp*]: Don't recite the whole prayer. Let's go straight to the most vital part: "Give us this day our daily bread."

BRECHTOLL: What must I do?

TRIPP: "Give us this day our daily bread."

3rd BROTHER *to Tripp*]: So that's you served.

TARABAS *to Brechtoll*]: The door is almost ajar. All that's needed is to . . .

BRECHTOLL: . . . make some concession? Which one? [*The Third Brother makes as if to go away with his trolley.*]

3rd BROTHER *to Tarabas, looking as if he is about to go*]: I think Mr. Tripp's had his portion already.

TRIPP *to the 3rd Brother*]: Brother, my soup.

TARABAS *to Brechtoll*]: You're eaten up with pride. It is not a question of making concessions, but of trying an experiment. Ask God. [*Approbation from the Black Side. To Tripp:*] Do you want a second helping? You're too greedy, Mr. Tripp. You should leave some for those who *don't* believe in God too, those whom God does *not* feed. Or perhaps you haven't been served, after all? [*To Brechtoll:*] Try the experiment! Ask the Good Lord for your soup!

BRECHTOLL: When I don't believe in Him!

TARABAS *to Tripp*]: Your soup and your daily bread, have

you had it or not? [*Mocking laughter from the Red Side. To the Third Brother*:] Has he been given his soup? [*To Brechtoll*:] You don't believe in Him. Try all the same. Pray to God. [*To Tripp*:] Answer me! That's an order. Have you had your food, yes or no?

TRIPP: No, Sir, no, Brother, I have not had my soup or my daily bread.

TARABAS *to Brechtoll*]: Perhaps He will give you proof of His existence. Perhaps you will have some success with Him. With me you have none. [*To Tripp*]: Perhaps he hasn't heard you, you didn't speak loud enough. Try again! [*To Brechtoll*:] Make up your mind, while you've still a little strength left to pray . . . [*Silence from Brechtoll.*] . . . before it's too late.

3rd BROTHER *to Tripp*]: You were asked to try again.

TARABAS *to Brechtoll*]: You hesitate, Mr. Brechtoll?

3rd BROTHER *to Tripp*]: Try again: This time it will work.

BRECHTOLL: I refuse. [*Rhythmical applause from the Red Side; disapproval from the Black side.*]

TARABAS: The rights of men! No soup, no freedom for the dogmatic.

3rd BROTHER *to Tripp*]: So you've no more faith in Him?

2nd BROTHER *to Brechtoll*]: You won't give in, will you? You won't give in, will you? [*The last two questions are also put by* JEAN *from his seat.*)

3rd BROTHER *to Tripp*]: Try again!

BRECHTOLL: What must I do?

TARABAS *to Brechtoll*]: Just a short prayer, I told you. A simple little prayer. You can judge for yourself how effective it is.

JEAN *to Brechtoll*]: . . . How effective it is . . . how effective it is . . .

TRIPP *kneeling down*]: Our Father . . .

86

BRECHTOLL: What prayer?

TARABAS *to Tripp*]: Louder! [*To Brechtoll*:] What it is not to know! On your knees!

TRIPP: Our Father, give me my daily bread!

3rd BROTHER *to Tripp*]: Not clear enough.

TARABAS *to Brechtoll*]: Don't turn towards me! I'm only a poor Brother. On your knees! Face that way! [*Brechtoll turns towards the audience.*]

TRIPP: Give me my daily bread, oh God!

TARABAS *to Brechtoll, who has fallen on his knees*]: Now clasp your hands!

BRECHTOLL: This is the first time I . . .

2nd BROTHER *to Brechtoll*]: It's easy. Like this.

TARABAS *to Tripp*]: Are you in the correct position? [*To the Two Brothers*:] Are their hands properly clasped? [*To Brechtoll*:] Don't get up again! Link your fingers! Don't be ashamed! He is the only one who sees you, apart from me and these two Brothers, all very discreet.

BRECHTOLL: I can't do it.

2nd BROTHER *to Brechtoll*]: No soup, then.

TARABAS *to Tripp*]: Perfect. Hands properly clasped. Eyes to Heaven. That's the prescribed attitude, all right. It's a habit you've obviously acquired.

2nd BROTHER *to Tarabas, indicating Brechtoll*]: He won't do it.

TARABAS *to Brechtoll*]: No soup. The door of the cage won't be opened either. Come on, make up your mind, damn you, pray! Don't bow your head like that! Courage! Eyes to Heaven! [*To Tripp*:] Concentrate and gather more strength before you try again.

BRECHTOLL: Heaven?

TARABAS: I mean: look at the ceiling.

BRECHTOLL: What a sinister farce! . . .

TARABAS: Don't be rude! Why do you try to annoy us? And

again, what can it matter to you if it succeeds? An experiment is an experiment. On your knees! Like that. Don't move! [*To Tripp*:] Have you concentrated enough?

BRECHTOLL: I'm hungry.

2nd BROTHER: That's the idea. You tell *Him* you're hungry.

BRECHTOLL: I'm hungry.

2nd BROTHER: *(to Brechtoll)*: I'm hungry, who? Name Him.

TRIPP: Give me my daily bread.

BRECHTOLL: God, I'm hungry.

TRIPP: Oh God!

BRECHTOLL *to Tarabas*]: Are you satisfied? I've said what I had to . . .

TARABAS *to Brechtoll*]: That's not the way you should speak to Him. There are certain conventions, the method, etiquette, there's the formula . . .

BRECHTOLL: The formula?

JEAN *from his seat*]: What formula? [*His face expresses the torment of Brechtoll and Tripp.*]

TARABAS *to Tripp*]: Am I deaf? Have you lost your voice? Louder! [*To Brechtoll*:] If you've forgotten it, we'll teach it you again.

TRIPP: Give me my daily bread, oh God.

TARABAS *to Brechtoll*]: It's so easy. Repeat after me: "Our Father which art in Heaven." [*To Tripp*:] Louder!

TRIPP *loud*]: "Our Father which art in Heaven, give us our daily bread."

BRECHTOLL: "Our Father which art in Heaven."

TARABAS *to Brechtoll and to Tripp*]: Louder and clearer still! Again!

BRECHTOLL and TRIPP *together*]: "Our Father which art in Heaven, Our Father which art in Heaven."

TARABAS *to Tripp*]: You're too tense. Be more relaxed! [*To Brechtoll*:] Put more warmth, more conviction into the phrase.

BRECHTOLL: Our Father which art in Heaven . . .

TRIPP: Our Father which art in Heaven . . .

BRECHTOLL: Give us our daily bread.

TARABAS: You admit you believe in God.

TRIPP *shouting louder and louder*]: Our Father which art in Heaven, give us our daily bread. Our Father which art in Heaven, give us our daily bread.

[JEAN *has spoken the last five speeches at the same time as* TRIPP *and* BRECHTOLL. *This may be punctuated by rhythmical applause from those on the Red Side and those on the Black Side, as at the Théâtre National Populaire.*]

TARABAS *to Brechtoll*]: Do you believe? Do you believe?

2nd BROTHER *to Brechtoll*]: Do you believe? Do you believe?

TARABAS *to Brechtoll, while Tripp goes on saying "Our Father" louder and louder*]: You hate me. You've no more strength to smash everything up. You can't even *stand* up. You can't unclasp your hands. You have just enough strength left to answer . . . Do you believe, yes or no?

BRECHTOLL *feebly*]: I believe.

TARABAS *to Brechtoll*]: I can't hear you. Articulate properly! Is the aroma of the soup filling the cage?

BRECHTOLL: Yes.

TARABAS *to Brechtoll*]: You see: you've been touched by divine mercy already. One little effort. What, who do you believe in?

BRECHTOLL: I believe in God.

TARABAS *to Tripp*]: A fine voice for a starving man! . . . Do you feel you've been fed by now?

TRIPP: Stop this game!

TARABAS *to Tripp*]: Oh no! Let us pray together. [*To Brechtoll*:] As you now believe, just say after me: "Our Father which art in Heaven" . . .

BRECHTOLL: Our Father which art in Heaven . . .

3rd BROTHER *to Tripp*

                  together]: Give us our daily bread.

2nd BROTHER *to Brechtoll*

2nd BROTHER *to Brechtoll*

                  together]: Our Father which **art in**

3rd BROTHER *to Tripp*   Heaven . . .

TARABAS: Give us our daily bread, our daily bread.

JEAN *from his seat, together with the Red and the Black **Sides**, rhythmically and beating time by clapping their hands*]: **Our** daily . . . bread . . . our . . . daily . . . bread . . .

TRIPP: Give us our bread!

BRECHTOLL: Our Father which art in Heaven.

TARABAS: Oh God, give Trip his daily bread! Do give it to Tripp! [*To Brechtoll:*] That's it. Here's your soup. Your prayers have been granted. There's your proof He **exists**. [*The Second Brother holds out a bowl to Brechtoll through the bars, which the latter falls upon.*]

[*Reaction from the Black Side, approving murmurs, as though yet another fresh fact had confirmed their faith.*]

3rd BROTHER: Lord, give Mr. Tripp his daily bread. Mr. Tripp, who is one of your faithful, is about to **starve to** death.

TARABAS *to Brechtoll*]: Isn't this wholesome material **proof of** His existence, of the efficacity of prayer?

BRECHTOLL: After this . . . I'll get my freedom too? [*He eats.*]

TARABAS *to Tripp*]: Still nothing to get your teeth into? Could it be that He's deaf? Does He want to punish you? Has He run out of victuals? These jokes of mine are unseemly, aren't they? Are you still hoping for your providential soup? In your place, I wouldn't be too sure.

TRIPP: Lord, why have you forsaken me? Why do you leave me in their hands? Why don't you spirit this **cage away**?

Why do you let me suffer from hunger? Why don't you carry me off? Oh God, why do you forsake me?

TARABAS *to the 3rd Brother, but looking at Tripp*]: Can He forsake his most faithful of servants?

3rd BROTHER: I don't think so. It must be an oversight.

JEAN *from his seat*]: He can't have forsaken him, it's not possible.

TRIPP: No, it isn't, is it? He won't forsake me?

TARABAS *to Tripp*]: He certainly wouldn't, if He existed. Does He exist? Answer! There's still some sou-soup left.

TRIPP: I think He exists.

TARABAS *to Tripp*]: You won't get any soup then. [*To Brechtoll:*] It's good to see you eating with such an appetite. *I didn't want to give you anything to eat. It's He* [*looking towards Heaven and pointing to the ceiling:*] *it's He who ordered me to give you your daily bread. In the soup, He even made that clear. Bread soup.* [*To Tripp:*] Do you believe in God?

TRIPP: I believe in God.

TARABAS *to Tripp*]: No soup then. [*To Brechtoll:*] It was His voice all right. [*To Tripp:*] Do you believe in God?

TRIPP: I believe.

TARABAS: No soup then. Do you believe in God? I feel you do. No soup then. [*To Brechtoll:*] When He gave me that order, I was bound to obey. He doesn't let His faithful starve to death.

TRIPP: Don't let me starve to death.

TARABAS: Do you believe in God?

TRIPP: Yes.

TARABAS: No soup then. [*The "no soup then" is taken up in chorus by the Red Side.*] Do you believe in God, Mr. Tripp? You don't want to answer? No soup. [*Again repeated by the Red Side.*]

91

TRIPP: I believe in Him. [*Muttered disapproval from the Red Side. Jean looks distractedly from one Side to the other.*]

TARABAS *to Brechtoll*]: He is omnipotent. He forced my hand. Would you like some more?

3rd BROTHER *to Tripp*]: No soup. I'm going to take some to those who are really hungry.

VOICE *from the Red Side*]: Yes, yes!..

TRIPP *on the floor*]: Don't leave me, Sir.

TARABAS *to Tripp*]: You should say: "Brother, pal, comrade."

TRIPP: Don't leave me, Friend, I'm ill, I'm hungry.

TARABAS *to Brechtoll*]: So, you really believe in God now, [*To Tripp:*] Do you still believe in God, Mr. Tripp?

TRIPP: Perhaps. A little . . .

JEAN *in a murmur*]: Perhaps. A little.

BRECHTOLL *eating*]: Yes, yes, I believe in Him. A little, perhaps . . .

3rd BROTHER *to Tripp*]
    speaking together]:
2nd BROTHER *to Brechtoll*]

That's not a clear answer. [*To Tarabas:*] No soup? [*Tarabas signals "no" with his hand.*] That's not a clear answer. [*To Tarabas:*] Shall I take his bowl away? [*Various reactions from the Red and Black Sides.*]

TARABAS *to Tripp*]: Come now, do you believe in God, Mr. Tripp?

TRIPP: I don't know, I don't know any more . . .

TARABAS *to Tripp*]: Give a modest answer, yes or no. It's so simple.

3rd BROTHER *to Tripp*]: Do you believe in God, Mr. Tripp? Do you believe in God?

TARABAS *to Brechtoll*]: It's so simple. Answer clearly, yes or no. Do you believe in God, Brechtoll? Do you believe in

God, Tripp?

BRECHTOLL: Yes, I believe in God. [*Approval from the Black Side.*]

TRIPP: No, I don't believe in God. [*Approval from the Red Side.*]

TARABAS *to the Brother Superior*]: Did you hear, Brother Superior? [*To Tripp and to Brechtoll*]: You're asked to be so kind as to repeat it.

TRIPP: No, I don't believe in God, no, I don't believe in God, no, I don't believe in God. [*The last "I don't believe . . ." is also said by Jean and the Red Side.*)

BRECHTOLL: Yes, I believe in God. Yes, I believe in God. [*The last "I believe in God" is repeated by Jean and the Black Side.*]

TARABAS: Don't stay on your knees to eat! What *do* you believe in, Mr. Tripp?

TRIPP: I believe in my soup. Give me my soup!

BRECHTOLL: I believe in God. Don't take my soup and my freedom away.

3rd BROTHER *to Tripp*]: Are you quite sure? You're not making a mistake?

TRIPP: I believe in my soup. [*Tarabas makes a sign to the Third Brother.*]

3rd BROTHER *to Tripp*]: Here it is! Here's that good soup! [*He offers Tripp a full bowl, which the latter falls upon.*]

BRECHTOLL *eating*]: I believe in God. You'll open the gates, won't you, as soon as I've built up my strength? Won't you?

TARABAS *to Tripp*]: And what sort of soup do you believe in?

TRIPP: I believe in good soup.

TARABAS *to Brechtoll and to Tripp*]: Your freedom . . . We'll talk about that again, one of these days. I don't know if there's a formula for regaining your freedom. I promise you I'll find out. It's possible, after all, that there may be one . . . [*Tripp and Brechtoll eat. To Jean, who has risen and gone up to Tarabas:*] How did you find me in this part? Did the show bore you? What do you think of the production?

JEAN: Very good, why yes, yes . . . Brother Tarabas. You're an excellent actor.

TARABAS: This is only the first episode, there are another twenty-nine. Total drama needs stamina. We won't show you the rest, unless you're particularly anxious . . . [*Jean makes some negative signs.*] No, you'd rather not . . . haven't the time . . . Anyway, for your information . . . in the next episode, as suggested by the character I was playing, they go off freedom . . . get disintoxicated. We demystify, forgive this hackneyed expression, the idea of winning one's freedom back, we demystify freedom itself . . .

JEAN: That's interesting. Thank you, thank you. I feel quite weak at the knees . . .

TARABAS *clapping his hands in the direction of Tripp and Brechtoll*]: That's it. The scene's over. [*The Brothers Tripp and Brechtoll have given their bowls back to go out with their trolleys, then return to the back of the stage and stand round Jean and Tarabas. Tripp and Brechtoll turn towards the supposed audience, that is to say towards Jean, and bow to him.*
The Red and Black members of the audience applaud. They stand up and either go out or take up a position right or left. Perhaps one Brother on each side will serve them something to nibble . . . rolls or refreshments . . .]

JEAN: The two clowns are extraordinary . . . my dear fellow . . . what technique! Congratulations . . . Once again, bravo! [*The two cages disappear with Tripp and Brechtoll inside. Later, perhaps, these two will appear again, as monks, at the end of the act. The tiers of seats disappear too; Jean's chair is removed.*]

TARABAS *continuing*]: My clowns have specialised in that kind of part.

JEAN: When you entertain visitors and want to do them the honour, the full honours, of putting on this show, do you always have the same two actors to play the prisoners? Always acting the same thing, surely they must get tired?

TARABAS: They never have enough. One day, perhaps they will. We've anticipated that. So, as they've each learnt the two parts, we put them in alternate cages. Brechtoll plays Tripp. Tripp plays Brechtoll.

JEAN: Gentlemen, Brothers, I'm eternally grateful to you for your welcome, for this magnificent show.

TARABAS: We've got thousands like it. And in quite different styles. Once again, I don't want to press you, but don't hesitate if you'd like to see more.

JEAN: Thank you, it would give you too much trouble.

2nd BROTHER: Trouble?

3rd BROTHER: Trouble? Why did you say trouble? [*To Jean:*] It was for *our* pleasure and for *your* pleasure. Why use the word "trouble"? Did you find anything unpleasant in it?

JEAN: No, not at all. That's not what I meant. I used the word "trouble" rather than any other, it just came to me automatically. It's "pleasure" I meant to say. It gave us all pleasure. So much pleasure that we've had enough.

3rd BROTHER: The words we use are revealing. The words that come spontaneously are the very ones that express our secret tendencies, our way of looking at things, our personality.

TARABAS: You've recovered now, you're rested. We've made you very welcome, haven't we, in our establishment? You must be pleased?

JEAN: Why yes, of course, I'm extremely grateful for your welcome. You have a delightful place. What panache, what style! I feel far better than I did. Thank you so much. Now I'd like to be on my way again.

TARABAS: We're bound to render each other some little service. We're human beings. We have obligations towards one another, unless we prefer the cage of solitude. But that's not a comfortable place. You can't quite stand up or sit down properly there.

JEAN *pointing to the Brothers who have just arrived, together with the Clowns, who are putting hoods over their heads so as to resemble the others; they will all take their seats on either side of a long table. During the ensuing speeches they walk slowly across the stage and go and sit down next to each other*]: Those are the actors? I mean the amateur actors, aren't they?

TARABAS: We're all amateur actors, but Brothers by profession.

JEAN: I know. You're right. Thank you. I'll be on my way again. To see what I didn't see before.

2nd BROTHER *to Tarabas*]: He hasn't really recovered yet. He's not been cured.

3rd BROTHER: That's my opinion too: he didn't enjoy the show. He probably even found it distasteful.

TARABAS: As you feel quite able to resume your journey, you're perfectly free to go.

JEAN: Yes, yes, I must. I'd like to see all I missed because of my failing sight. I've some crucial experiences still to come. The beauty I never noticed. I'm sorry about that word: this time, Brother, you'll be saying it reveals something or other I'm trying to hide, or some untidy thinking on my part . . . or Heaven knows what, hundreds of things . . . I haven't discovered the essential yet. But I have regained my strength. I must say goodbye. Give you my best wishes. Thank you again: tell me what I owe you, please make out the bill!

TARABAS: It's not much. It can't amount to much.

JEAN: Did you find my story interesting?

TARABAS *turning towards the Brother Superior*]: Our guest's story . . . his story . . . Very good, Brother Superior. [*To Jean:*] In terms of money, it didn't carry much weight, from what our Brother Superior was given to understand by our Brother Accountant.

3rd BROTHER: It's certainly not worth its weight in gold.

JEAN: Tell me anyway, tell me what I owe you so I can be on my way. [*Short pause.*] Right. Obviously, what I told you wasn't very interesting, I realise that. But there's one thing I didn't confess to you. It's not that I wanted to hide it, it was just that I forgot.

2nd BROTHER *looking at the Brother Superior*]: Hiding? And forgetting? . . . It all comes to the same.

JEAN: Everything I wished for would vanish at my approach, everything I tried to touch would wither. As soon as I wandered into some sunny meadow, clouds would cover the sky. I was never able to take delight in anything. The grass wilted beneath my feet, before my eyes the leaves on the trees turned yellow and fell to earth. If I tried to drink the clearest of spring water it would taste brackish, nauseating.

3rd BROTHER: That's why he was always thirsty.

2nd BROTHER: Thirsty for everything. Disgusted with everything too. [*Jean goes towards the door where the monk with the carbine is stationed and the latter blocks the way. He goes to the back of the stage where the bars stand out against a grey background, that is to say the deserted plain. . . He comes back.*]

TARABAS: So you've always been a prey to this insatiable thirst, to some hunger you cannot assuage?

JEAN: Yes . . . No . . . Why yes . . . After all, why not tell you everything? Can I really remember? Am I inventing? It seems to me I haven't always been swept by this consuming fire. Once upon a time, such a long time ago, yes, perhaps before or right at the start of my journey, no, I rather think it was before, that's right, before, when the days were luminous, I'd stop in the heart of the countryside, and it was as if I was at the centre of the universe. Then I'd swivel round and look about me . . . lost in unspeakable wonder and delight I'd shout and cry: "It's fantastic! Out of this world! It's incredible and yet it *is* out of this world, that forest or those simple bushes, that road going up and up, that street, those three or four houses, or that procession, that lake or that expanse of sea!" Or else I'd sit down in the tall grass, and just gaze about intently, blissfully happy. Everything was complete, sufficient unto itself. I wasn't hungry. I wasn't thirsty, or rather this joy was my bread and water. Why this sudden change? This sudden deprivation? Can you explain that, Brother Tarabas? Can you explain, Brothers? Can you, Brother Superior? Why this sudden hunger, this sudden thirst? This dissatisfaction and the anguish, why, suddenly, this hollow feeling inside me, that's grown bigger and deeper ever since? This gaping void I've never been able to fill? Why were there no more luminous days, why this gloom? Was I meant to endure it? Was I meant to resign myself? Was I meant to wait? Was I meant to expect nothing? Was I or was I not meant to roam those twilit autumn roads in search of light . . . or one of those mirages?

3rd BROTHER: He had talents, though.

4th BROTHER: He kept them to himself.

5th BROTHER *ex Tripp*]: They've stagnated inside him, they've

98

corroded.

6th BROTHER *ex Brechtoll*]: They became ulcerated, gangrenous.

3rd BROTHER: It would have been so easy for him to find relief.

2nd BROTHER: They become a disease.

JEAN: I cried out. I shouted. No-one came to my aid. One word perhaps would have done. But I'll take up my travels again. I must go in search of land that won't burn me, water that won't engulf me, a bush that has no thorns.

3rd BROTHER *to the Brother Superior*]: Does that count as something extra? [*Stubborn silence from the Brother Superior.*]

TARABAS *turning towards the Brother Superior, who is still silent*]: We can't take your last declaration into account.

JEAN: I must go. I must go on searching. Tell me, Brothers, what I owe you. I'm in a hurry. [*He rummages through his pockets, takes his hand out again and shows that it is open and empty.*] This dirt is all the change I've got. That's all I could accumulate on this trip. On *this* trip . . . I've bloodstains on my fingers too, the blood I drew when I got caught on the brambles . . . Still, it's only a tiny little scratch.

TARABAS: Don't worry! We're not ordinary inn-keepers! We're not in business, we don't take money. We don't take the blood of our clients as surety. We don't exact contributions. You should, however, discharge your debt, only in a different way. You will, if you don't mind, do us a little service. Then you will be free to go. No, no, it won't take long. Tell us first if you're satisfied, if the food was good, if you've been well entertained.

JEAN: Of course. Thank you with all my heart. Tell me what I must do. How can I prove my gratitude . . . how can I

99

discharge my debt, morally? [*Tarabas turns his head towards the Brother Superior, then again towards Jean: the Brother Superior goes quietly off on the audience's left. The back of the stage lights up: through the bars you can see Marie-Madeleine and Marthe. The set, behind the bars, represents the garden of the final scene of the First Act "The Flight": luminous, with a blue sky, vegetation, trees in blossom and the ladder hanging in the same place. Very intense light, deep blue. Marthe is wearing a pale dress, Marie-Madeleine a blue suit with a red carnation in her button-hole. The lines on her face have disappeared and she seems very young.*]

MARIE *behind the bars*]: Jean, we're here, we're waiting for you.

JEAN: My darlings! Oh my darlings!

MARIE: Come and join us, then! Look what a lovely day it is! [*She indicates Marthe:*] She was in her cradle when you left. Now she's fifteen.

JEAN: I remember.

MARIE: You see how tall she is. Would you have thought she'd have grown so beautiful?

JEAN: I still recognise her. My heart does. I'd stopped hoping I'd see you again. How happy I am now! Perhaps I should never have gone away. So you're really here. But the other one, that other one, she for whom I was neither father, nor son, nor husband?

MARIE: Come.

JEAN: In a few minutes, I can't come for a moment. I've got to pay for my food. I must repay them. It won't take long.

MARIE: Hurry up! Springtime is short. You know that. It comes back again, that's certain, but it's dreary waiting for it.

JEAN *to Tarabas*]: What do I have to do to settle my debt?

TARABAS: This strikes you as a prison here. It isn't. The Brothers you can see sitting at table may look mournful.

But if that's what you think you're wrong. They're not any more. They may look tortured. Yet there is no torture here. It may seem like melancholy. In fact it's serenity.

JEAN: You'd think they were dragging chains.

TARABAS: Look again. They haven't any. What gave you that idea? You must have hallucinations. We don't ill-treat them. They're sheltered from the sunshine and the rain. Protected from war and poverty. Our surgeons eradicated those germs of conflict in them which were ruining their health.

MARIE: Hurry up, come on!

JEAN: It won't take me long. Is the other one coming? [*To Tarabas*:] It won't take long, will it? [*To Marthe and Marie-Madeleine*:] I'd never noticed the light all round you before; you've always been in that light. I hadn't realised. In a moment I'll be with you and I won't leave you again in a hurry. Can you see the third one arriving in the distance? You ought to be able to pick her out. I'm coming, I'm coming, I'm coming! How I want to hold you in my arms! Just when I thought I'd lost you! I can't wait to kiss you. I'm so longing to kiss you. [*To Tarabas*:] Will it take long?

TARABAS: Patience, Brother Jean, patience. Don't get excited. For one moment . . . or for two moments, you're going to take the place of one of our absent Brothers.

JEAN *to Marthe and Marie-Madeleine*]: I'm coming! She must be coming too? Can you see her?

TARABAS: Would you like to be the warder of the dungeons? [*Jean shakes his head.*] That's not for you. You don't want to be the warder of anything. Would you like to be charged with attendance on the dying?

JEAN: No, no.

TARABAS: That's not for you, no. You don't want to do the

cooking, either. [*Jean shakes his head.*] Right. Good. We
won't ask you to carry heavy loads. We've got labourers
and carriers. Rest assured we won't send you after the
gold buried in the mines beneath the building. You won't
be looking after the accounts, the administrative business
or the trials. No. We'll spare you all that, of course. Still,
after all, we've got to find you something. No-one is
excused some social service. So there, don't worry, we'll
decide for you. That'll be best. All for the best. As everyone eats and everyone drinks, as we do nothing but that,
it's easy to find you a job: we'll ask you to serve a meal to
our Brothers sitting round the table, our Brothers, who
look like miserable tramps, not because they're not well
fed, but because they're always famished, like you. You
know what it's like. After you've waited at table, you can
go and rejoin your family.

JEAN *to Marie and Marthe*]: My loved ones . . .

TARABAS: In the meadow, among the beauties of Nature's
scenery. You mustn't blame us if we ask you this little
favour in exchange. It's so *you'll* feel more at ease. A small
exchange, isn't it? Not asking too much of you? It's
normal, the usual practice.

JEAN: Just tell me how long it will take. How long, how long?
[*To Marie-Madeleine and Marthe*]: I'll soon finish, then I'll
come. Yes, we'll hold each other by the hand, and we'll
sing and dance through the fields, dance along . . . all
keeping time together. Wait for me, tell her to wait too, if
you see her!

TARABAS: How long? It's hard to tell.

JEAN: Tell me, all the same.

TARABAS: We'll have to work it out.

MARIE: The springtime you love . . .

JEAN *to Marthe and Marie*]: Wait for me! I love *you* above everything. The tenderness I feel for you towers above the mountain-tops. I've always loved you, now I understand. [*To Tarabas:*] Tell me, Brother, tell me! Work it out more quickly. When will I be able to go? [*Through the opening in the wall, a hand passes out bowls, one after the other, and cutlery, a pot of soup, a ladle. Jean begins serving the Brothers at table while the Second Brother dresses him in a monk's habit. Reaction from Jean.*]

TARABAS: It won't be difficult to do. Just wait on them at table, no cooking to be done. The dishes are all ready. These Brothers aren't like the clowns just now, they're really getting something good to eat. This isn't the theatre any more. [*Jean looks as though he wants to take off his monk's habit.*]

2nd BROTHER: It's so you won't dirty your clothes, Brother Jean, you've got to look nice for your walk.

JEAN *to Tarabas*]: Reckon it up more quickly please, I'm in a hurry. They're here, waiting for me. Someone else may come too. Tell me, how many seconds? How many minutes? Work it out in minutes, I don't mind by the minute. How many minutes more do I have to stay? How many do I owe? How many minutes is the meal going to last?

TARABAS: You want me to work out in minutes the amount of time you owe us? In minutes? That's not one of my tasks. It's the Brother Accountant who makes these calculations. And *he's* had his instructions from the Brother Superior. [*To the Brother Accountant:*] How many minutes does our Brother Jean owe us? [*Silence from the Brother Accountant. The Second Brother puts the hood over Jean's head.*]

2nd BROTHER: It's so the smell of cooking doesn't get in your hair.

JEAN: All right. I see it's too difficult to work it out in

103

minutes. In hours is really more convenient. How many hours of service do I owe you?

TARABAS: Tell him, Brother Accountant, work it out! Tell him so he knows exactly and set his mind at rest. For his family's sake too.

JEAN *in the direction of the bars*]: I'll tell you how many hours I'll be . . . Wait for me at the gates! Wait for me at the windows! Wait for me on the roads! Wait for me in the houses! Wait! Stay where I can see you! Go on waiting! And make her wait, too! They're just going to tell me now!

3rd BROTHER: Meanwhile, you must do your own waiting. Wait at table, on all these hungry people. Don't waste time! Start serving! You must see their platters are always kept full.

TARABAS *to the Brother Accountant*]: Tell him the number of hours he owes us!

MARIE: We're here!

MARTHE: Waiting for you!

MARIE: We'll wait! That'll help you! Don't forget we're waiting!

JEAN: I think that *will* help me. I've lived through worse moments than this. It will pass. I hope and believe it will. [*He starts serving again. To the Brother Accountant:*] Brother Accountant, what's the total number of hours I owe you? What's the final total? Please tell me, quickly!

MARIE: We'll wait for you, my darling! No matter how long, we'll wait!

BROTHER ACCOUNTANT: The number of hours due to us from our Brother Jean for the provision at our inn of board and lodging, entertainment and attendance at one lecture, is as follows: one, three, six, seven, eight, nine . . .

[*On the blackboard which appears near the bars the Third Brother writes the figures in chalk as they are being spoken.*]

104

. . . one, seven, three, six, nine, eight, one, seven, three, six
nine, eight . . .

[*All the Brothers take it up in chorus, as the figures appear on
the blackboard, then on screens that also appear and light up
simultaneously in different parts of the stage and on the walls.
Followed by the others, who repeat his words like an echo, he
continues:*]

One, seven, three, six, nine, eight, [*then, faster and faster:*]
One, seven, three, six, nine, eight, [*then faster and faster still.
It is taken up in chorus by Brother Tarabas and the men at the
table, and also by the two women, who repeat the figures with more
signs of alarm. The figures go on lighting up, as the monk's hand
passes the bowls and the cutlery out to Jean in rhythmically
staccato style. Meanwhile Jean goes on serving setting down the
bowls etc. . . . and picking them up again to carry them to the
hatch, where he fetches more and so on:*]

one, seven, three, six, nine, eight, one, seven, three, six,
nine, eight, one, seven, three, six, nine, eight, one, seven,
three, six, nine, eight, one, seven, three, six, nine, eight,
one, seven, three, six, nine, eight, one, seven, three, six,
nine, eight, one, seven, three, six, nine, eight, one, seven,
three, six, nine, eight, one, seven, three, six, nine, eight,
one, seven, three, six, nine, eight, one, seven, three, six,
nine, eight, one, seven, three, six, nine, eight, one, seven,
three, six, nine, eight, one, seven, three, six, nine, eight,
one, seven, three, six, nine, eight . . . etc. . . . etc. . . .

[*On the blackboard and on the walls, the figures go on piling up
indefinitely and stretch round on all sides. Brother Tarabas
repeats them too, stressing them more emphatically.*]

TARABAS: Go on, go on! Do your stint. Look after our
Brothers even better than they looked after you. Go on,
you're young! Go on, go on! [*Jean too repeats the figures while
he is pouring soup out into the bowls or platters, still to a set*

rhythm.]

MARIE: We'll wait! We'll wait! No matter how long, I'll wait for you, I'll wait for you for ever! [*The chorus continues: one, seven, three, six, nine, eight, one, seven, three, six, nine, eight, one, seven, three, six, nine, eight . . . The saying of the last figures is accompanied by a bell or several bells that strike the hours. Jean goes on serving at an ever-increasing pace, in the same rhythmically staccato style.*]

CURTAIN

THE PICTURE

Characters

THE LARGE GENTLEMAN

THE PAINTER

ALICE

THE NEIGHBOUR

THE SET

A big room with one very big desk as the only piece of furniture. A leather armchair in front of the desk, in which the LARGE GENTLE-MAN *is sitting.*

A door on the right, another on the left; a window in the right-hand corner.

The LARGE GENTLEMAN *is expensively but tastelessly dressed. He is in his shirtsleeves; his jacket is hanging over the armchair. The* PAINTER *is very poorly dressed and ill-shaven; he might almost be taken for a tramp. He is wearing a loosely-tied cravat and carrying his canvas rolled up under his arm.*

ALICE *is a very old woman, with a dirty apron, and clumsy shoes or dirty slippers. She has untidy hair, wears glasses, walks with a white stick and has only one arm; she sniffs a great deal.*

The PAINTER *is excessively shy and looks rather simple.*

When the Curtain rises the LARGE GENTLEMAN *is sitting at his desk. He is constantly looking at his wrist-watch and fingering his many-coloured tie.*

Facing him, near the right-hand door, the PAINTER *is standing at a respectful distance.*

THE PICTURE

LARGE GENTLEMAN: Come closer, step right up . . . [*The Painter does not move.*] You see, it took me a long time to get under way. No, it wasn't easy. The problems that faced me were insoluble, but I managed to solve them; and yet that wasn't the end of my troubles. Believe me, there are no such things as miracles: I'm sure you realize that.

PAINTER: Yes sir, I realize that.

LARGE G: I'm a bulldog, so I stuck to it, never let go. You

see, all that really matters is to hang on like grim death.

PAINTER: Like grim death, yes, sir.

LARGE G: Nothing falls from Heaven all prepared and ready to eat, like manna in the wilderness. [*With a sweeping movement of the arm to take in the room, the desk and himself.*] Glance around and you'll see the result of my labours, all this is mine. What do you think of it, eh? Tell me what you think of it.

PAINTER: Why yes, indeed, I . . .

LARGE G. *mopping his brow*]: The fruit of my toil, the sweat of my brow. I'm proud of it.

PAINTER: Oh . . . you've every right to be.

LARGE G: Come closer. [*The Painter takes half a step forward.*] Yes, I've every right to be proud. I think I can say, without boasting, that others can learn from my example, and so can you. I'm not selfish about it, unlike most people who have reached the top as I have, through will-power, tenacity, energy and work. I just said there were no such things as miracles. Well, I was wrong. There is *one* miracle.

PAINTER: One miracle?

LARGE G: Yes. Don't misunderstand me. The one and only miracle, the supreme miracle—is work.

PAINTER: Yes, of course: the miracle of work.

LARGE G: There you are, you've said it yourself. I know I'm right. [*Once more indicating the walls and the desk.*] And the proof is all around me: my efforts materialized in *this house.*

PAINTER: No doubt about that. [*He shifts his canvas from one arm to the other.*]

LARGE G: *I* am a self-made man. Life for me has been one long struggle. Life is a pitiless battlefield, and you advance over the bodies of the fallen! I wonder if you agree.

PAINTER: Oh yes, sir! I do.

LARGE G: A pitiless battlefield . . . but a fair fight: the survival of the fittest.

PAINTER: Survival of the fittest, yes, sir.

LARGE G: And in the end it almost gives you a feeling of pleasure, a kind of deep and bitter satisfaction, the joy of a job well done . . . And you can sleep at night, with a quiet mind.

PAINTER: Quiet. Yes, sir.

LARGE G: But what sort of quiet is it? I'll tell you: it's the calm after the storm.

PAINTER: Oh yes, after . . . after the storm.

LARGE G: Come closer, closer. Since my early childhood I've had a very hard life. My father . . . but we won't speak of him; perhaps it wasn't entirely his fault, he's dead. So are my grandparents. As for my mother, she married again, married a drunkard. My father drank a lot too, but he was my father. While the other, how can I put it, was only my stepfather, and hardly *that!* Anyhow, my mother died too. [*Emotionally.*] You can't imagine what it is for a young chap, hurled into the jungle of life . . . but I came through.

PAINTER *getting emotional too*]: Yes, sir, I know.

LARGE G: No, no, my lad, you can't possibly imagine.

PAINTER: It was like that for me too . . . My mother . . .

LARGE G: No, my dear boy, no, it's not the same. We're all so different from one another.

PAINTER: Oh yes, that's true!

LARGE G: You see that window over the street. [*He motions the Painter to go to it.*] Go and look out, go on.

PAINTER *still with his rolled-up canvas, goes to the window*]: Here?

LARGE G: What can you see?

PAINTER: People passing.

LARGE G: What are they doing?

111

PAINTER: Just passing.

LARGE G: You're not very observant. Have another look. There aren't two of them alike.

PAINTER: No, I suppose there aren't.

LARGE G: I know. It's not the first time I've looked at them. I'm always watching them, when I'm not seeing people, in my moments of meditation.

PAINTER *coming back quietly to his first position, his canvas still under his arm*]: Yes, sir.

LARGE G: I can see them from the inside . . . do put your picture down! And yet they're all alike: that's the whole mystery of life . . . [*The Painter again shifts his picture from one arm to the other, there being nowhere for him to put it down.*] Must you keep on shifting that picture from side to side? It's not a rifle.

PAINTER: Very sorry, sir.

LARGE G: Sit down, my boy.

PAINTER *once more looking in vain for a seat*]: Yes, sir.

LARGE G: You see, my lad. I've twenty years of the Stock Exchange behind me. I gambled and I won. [*With a wave of the hand.*] Now I have the telephone.

[*The telephone rings.*]

And it works. That should convince you.

PAINTER: Yes, sir.

LARGE G: *I* don't want to convince you. You must feel convinced in yourself. The Stock Exchange toughens a man. The Stock Exchange is like life—you have to make up your mind and stick to it.

PAINTER: Yes, sir.

LARGE G. *almost sobbing*]: Many a night, old chap, I've spent on a bed of straw, in the workhouse, any old place; I educated myself, with no-one to help me; I've never felt really young.

PAINTER: Please don't cry, sir.

LARGE G: I live in this house, and it's my house, with my sister . . . She's a lot older than I am . . . And yet I've always had—believe me, I don't want to brag, you'll think I'm joking . . .

PAINTER: Oh no, sir! No!

LARGE G. *motioning him to keep quiet*]: I've always had a taste for the arts; good music, good books, good painting, films . . . Unfortunately I've never had much time for reading, for going to museums, concerts or theatres . . . We can never do what we want in life. [*Loudly*.] I tell you, when people say they do what they want in life, they don't know what they're talking about.

PAINTER: No, sir. Indeed they don't.

LARGE G: I was too tired in the evenings, after the Stock Exchange, as you'll easily understand; but I've the soul of an artist. Just to show you, old chap, that I don't in any way look down on creative artists, as perhaps you might be tempted to think, because I know what you're . . .

PAINTER: I . . . I wouldn't dream of such a thing!

LARGE G: Good for you, but why don't you pull up a chair?

[*The* PAINTER *reacts as before*.]

LARGE G: I don't in any way look down on creative artists; on the contrary I admire them, the good ones I mean, the real artists, the sincere ones . . . because you see [*With a broad smile*:] in art . . . and especially in painting . . . as you're a painter . . .

PAINTER *embarrassed*]: Oh, sir, I'm not a well-known . . .

LARGE G: . . . just as in business, you must have a professional conscience; otherwise it's no good. If you take my advice, *you* can turn your *art* into a way to get on in life. In its own fashion, art is as good a battlefield as anything else. Question of temperament. After all, it's happiness we're

113

each of us looking for; we're team mates sharing the same ideal; that's why, when all's said and done, men *can* get along together: any form of society must be founded on the common aims of its members. That is the principle of all humanism.

PAINTER: Ah! Humanism's a great thing.

[*For a few moments both are lost in reflection.*]

LARGE G: Why don't you pull up a chair and put your picture down?

[*The* PAINTER *reacts as before.*]

As you've let me talk to you so confidentially, I'm going to tell you everything. You don't mind, do you? I like confiding in people.

PAINTER: Oh no, of course not! It's an honour I was hardly expecting.

LARGE G: Very kind of you, thank you. I like confiding in people, but not just anybody, only those I can trust. I believe you are almost the first person . . .

PAINTER: I shall try, sir, to be worthy of the confidence you . . .

LARGE G: But you are. I know. I feel when I can trust someone. Now you've only just arrived, come to sell your picture.

PAINTER *shyly*]: Yes . . . if I could . . . I should like . . . very much . . .

LARGE G: And yet, you're not the first. You are—you know, old chap, I've got intuition, and that's what's brought me success—you are one of those noble creatures, so rare nowadays, who absorb things, who enjoy listening to others and sharing their troubles; I'm sure you are, how shall I say, I'm not mistaken, am I? . . .

PAINTER: I hope not, sir.

LARGE G: You are one of those people for whom others really exist; you're not a selfish man: selfish—that's the word.

114

PAINTER: Yes, that's the word.

LARGE G: Don't deny it . . . no false modesty . . . I'm not flattering you. I know it's the truth . . . I never tell a lie, my boy!

PAINTER: I never said that . . .

LARGE G: And so, at the end of this victorious struggle, which has made me what I am . . . which has helped me to achieve . . . [*Impressive gesture.*] I needn't repeat myself . . . all this, when the battle had ended in triumph, old chap, the battle that gave me everything . . . there was always something missing. Perhaps the one thing needful. [*He stands up.*] I am not a happy man. [*He sits down again.*]

PAINTER *sorry for him*]: Not happy, sir?

LARGE G: I'm afraid you'd never think that, would you? The human heart is so complicated! I'm hungry for beauty. It's missing from my life. I've never managed to satisfy my taste, I might almost say my passion, for the arts. In other fields I succeeded in everything, but I failed, for instance, to find a wife who could understand me, though of course, as you know, it's not easy.

PAINTER: No, indeed it isn't.

LARGE G: But is it really impossible?

PAINTER: Perhaps not really impossible.

LARGE G: Frankly, it *is* impossible.

PAINTER: You're right. It's impossible.

LARGE G: No, not *impossible*.

PAINTER: Well, perhaps not, after all.

LARGE G: No, no, I still can't believe it's really impossible. Anyway, we'll see. Just imagine, all the finest qualities of body and soul combined in *one* woman . . . who's intelligent, that's the word . . .

PAINTER: Yes, that's the word.

LARGE G: And lovely to look at . . . lovely. A beautiful woman who understands everything. But beautiful, old chap, above all she must be beautiful . . . Unfortunately such a woman has never crossed my path.

PAINTER *dreamily*]: The path of life . . .

LARGE G: At least I could have beauty reflected in the house. [*Sweeping gesture.*] These bare walls, believe me . . .

PAINTER: Oh, I do, sir.

LARGE G: These bare walls weigh me down.

PAINTER *indicating the canvas rolled up under his arm*]: Perhaps, perhaps you might like this picture . . . perhaps, in a way . . . it might . . .

LARGE G: I ask myself one question: can art take the place of the woman of my dreams, that good and beautiful woman, above all beautiful, I miss so much?

PAINTER: Try. Look and see. [*He shows the picture.*]

LARGE G: Of course, there's my sister. She's much older than I am, lives in this house, hasn't made much of her life, no harm in her, what would she do without me? I've given her a home, I look after all her needs, give her bed and board, she's in the kitchen now, takes care of me as best she can, does all the housework, I don't say she's not fond of me, but . . . well . . . I see you understand, sisterly affection, that's not what I'm after, it's not *that* . . .

PAINTER: No, it wouldn't be that . . .

LARGE G: Mind you, I'm not blaming her, not blaming her at all. And yet if she'd been beautiful, I'd have enjoyed looking at her. When I come home in the evening, tired of the ugliness of life, I'd like to be able to gaze at a beautiful face, a graceful figure . . . She's all I have, old chap, in life. And she's ugly.

PAINTER: What a shame!

LARGE G: Yes, my boy, it's unfortunate! But it wouldn't do any good to hide the truth.

PAINTER: Quite right, sir. Of course that wouldn't do any good.

LARGE G: And yet, you know, even my sister hasn't destroyed the deep desire for beauty inside me, no, she's made it more vital, more intense, [*Sigh.*] more poignant than ever . . . You can't imagine how poignant it is.

PAINTER *very sorry for him*]: I *do* understand, sir.

LARGE G: What I admire in you is your sympathy and understanding. You must be a genuine artist. From now on you have a place in my heart and in my home. We are friends.

PAINTER: Oh, I'm very flattered, very happy to . . .

LARGE G: You understand everything, straightaway. And yet there are so many people who don't understand my life at all and never even take the trouble to come and see me.

PAINTER: They *ought* to . . .

LARGE G: My sister's not by any means to be despised, she's not a bad sort, not entirely without a sense of beauty. But with her it's as if beauty were buried in the murky depths of the soul; her artistic impulse has been swallowed up in the dark waters of oblivion. It has to be fished out of her subconscious. My sister only lives, dear boy, in the world of necessity, she has no sense of humour, she forges her own chains, no freedom. I ask you, my boy, what are we without beauty and music and poetry . . . what would we be like, eh?

PAINTER: Er, we'd be, er . . .

LARGE G: Yes, I'm asking you, what would we be like?

PAINTER: Er . . . I . . . I don't know, sir.

LARGE G: Then I'll tell you . . .

   [*Banging his fist hard on the table.*]

   . . . brutes, sir.

PAINTER *slightly alarmed*]: Oh . . . perhaps not . . .

117

LARGE G: Yes, we would. Brutes! No doubt about it. Without beauty, no charity; without charity, no truth. It's all one and indivisible!

PAINTER: And yet, and yet . . .

LARGE G: And yet what? There's no 'and yet' about it, no contradiction possible; didn't you say just now that you understood me?

PAINTER: Yes, I understand you, sir.

LARGE G: Well then?

[*The* PAINTER *is rather embarrassed; he puts his picture under the arm.*]

Sit down, dear boy, sit down.

[*The* PAINTER *reacts as before.*]

She's dependent on me, I earn my living, of course, I'm in a position to feed another mouth.

PAINTER *weakly*]: Your sister's mouth, sir?

LARGE G: That's who we're talking about, isn't it? What's the matter with you?

PAINTER: I'm sorry, sir. I *was* listening.

LARGE G: Well, briefly, I've only one thing against her, and even *that*—you see, I think it's only fair to admit it—even *that* is not her fault. What I have against her is that she's no ornament in a house that's too plain, anyway, too bare, too grim . . . Otherwise, I wouldn't be buying pictures . . . I have to buy pictures because my sister's ugly, and that costs money.

PAINTER: Not really, sir, you know, a man like you . . .

LARGE G: Right, cards on the table, how much do you want?

PAINTER *taken by surprise, embarrassed*]: I . . . I . . . I don't know, sir . . .

LARGE G: What's your price? Give me a figure, but don't exceed the normal price for a masterpiece.

PAINTER *embarrassed*]: I only came here, sir, just to ask quite

simply . . . if you'd mind glancing at this picture . . . and if
you'd mind . . .

LARGE G: Talk, talk, talk! You came here to sell your goods,
didn't you? No more beating about the bush. As for me,
I've just told you, for the reasons I've just indicated I am,
or to be precise may eventually become, a buyer, pro-
viding your work satisfies certain aesthetic as well as
financial considerations, which are merely the expression
of my sincere and noble ideals in art and economics.

PAINTER *more and more embarrassed*]: Yes, sir, of course . . .
Naturally.

LARGE G: As far as finance is concerned, your figure will have
to be modest, and it's up to you to let me know the price;
as for the artistic quality of the work, which should be of
the highest order, I trust my own judgment.

PAINTER: To start with, just have a look at it, and you can
tell me afterwards if it interests you or not . . . The first
thing is to know if you like it.

LARGE G. *gets up and goes to the Painter, then sits down again*]:
It can only interest me if the price falls within certain
financial limits; it's a principle of mine, dear boy, believe
me, just a matter of principle.

PAINTER: Yes, sir, of course, I understand . . .

LARGE G: Glad you do.

PAINTER: And yet . . .

LARGE G: Yet what?

PAINTER *stammering*]: You must, I mean . . . Perhaps you
should . . . look first . . .

LARGE G: First, the price, my dear chap, aesthetics later.

PAINTER: It's all rather embarrassing. Just glance at it.

LARGE G: No. You can't teach me anything about embarrassing situations; I won't look until I've heard your practical
requirements. I've told you, it's a principle. You did say

you understood me, didn't you?

PAINTER: Oh yes, oh yes!

LARGE G: Well then. Your price?

PAINTER: Hm! Er . . . do you know . . .

LARGE G: What should I be knowing? What do you think I don't know yet?

PAINTER: Well, you must be aware . . . [*Making an effort.*] A painter of my type, a contemporary painter, for example Rembrandt or Rubens . . .

LARGE G: I don't know the gentlemen, though I'm not lacking in culture . . .

PAINTER: I'm quite sure you're not . . . Rembrandt or Rubens . . .

LARGE G: I hope it's not non-representational painting?

PAINTER: Oh no, sir. I have done some, but I'm past that stage now, I'm back to realistic subjects.

LARGE G: Glad to hear you've turned over a new leaf. Congratulations.

PAINTER: So, if you'll allow me . . . Rembrandt or Rubens would sell a picture like this . . . for 500,000 francs . . . I can let you have mine for 400,000.

LARGE G. *stupefied*]: 400,000 francs! You don't know the value of money! Poor fellow! Don't you realize that's a *fortune*? It's giving money away for the least effort. It's not every day that I earn a sum like that on the Stock Exchange! And I hope you now understand that the Stock Exchange is a desperate battle that wears a man out; a race won by the strongest runner . . . Whereas *you*, you just sit there quietly in front of your easel. No, my lad, no, 400,000 times no!

PAINTER: My work's not easy either, not everyone can do it.

LARGE G: Back to business.

PAINTER: I can offer it to you for 300,000 francs.

LARGE G: 3 or 400,000 it's almost the same.

PAINTER: For 250,000 . . . 200,000 . . .

LARGE G: 3 or 200,000, it's still the same.

PAINTER: 100,000.

LARGE G. *throwing up his arms*]: 100,000! 1 or 200,000 what's the difference?

PAINTER 80,000 . . . [*The Large Gentleman shakes his head.*] 70,000 . . . [*Shakes his head.*] 60,000 . .

LARGE G: Between 70 and 60, you know . . . [*Shakes his head.*]

PAINTER: 50,000 . . .

LARGE G: From 60,000 to 50,000's not much of a jump. Take a big one, my lad, take several.

PAINTER: But you must admit I've lowered my price considerably.

LARGE G: I admit nothing of the sort.

PAINTER *taking his courage in both hands*]: In that case, sir, I'm very sorry . . . I'd only be undervaluing my own work . . . [*With an effort.*] For I too have my principles . . .

LARGE G: Good for you. If you do have principles, keep them to yourself. And your picture too.

PAINTER: It's a pity, sir. Goodbye, sir! [*He makes for the door.*]

LARGE G. *almost begging*]: One moment! Look here, my dear chap, you're not going to leave me with these bare dirty walls, these ugly walls that torture me with their lack of beauty! Think again, think of others for once!

PAINTER *near the door, with a forced smile*]: Beauty, you know, has to be paid for, too . . .

LARGE G: Rubbish! An artist like you, the kind I hope you are, is not just a tradesman; he should be a priest who serves beauty, like the vestal virgins.

PAINTER: I have to live, sir.

LARGE G: What about me, don't I have to look after my sister? Please show a little human feeling . . .

PAINTER *coming back*]: Perhaps you're right.

LARGE G: I'm not asking you to offer it to me . . . for nothing. That'd make me angry. I don't want to be in anyone's debt.

PAINTER: I'll let you have it for 40,000 . . .

LARGE G: 14,000 francs? What an idea, that's far too much!

PAINTER: I said . . . I said . . . 40, not 14. 40,000 francs.

LARGE G: I'm neither deaf nor dumb. You said 14,000 francs!

PAINTER: Oh no, sir, I didn't: 40!

LARGE G: I see you're going back on your last word, which I couldn't accept anyway. You're not a man of honour: a man of honour is a man of his word.

PAINTER: 40, sir.

LARGE G: 14 . . .

PAINTER: I'm sorry: 40. I really did say: 40.

LARGE G: 40 what?

PAINTER: 40,000.

LARGE G. *dumbfounded*]: 40,000. [*Sarcastically.*] And you think I'm going to believe you? You won't catch me.

PAINTER: But . . .

LARGE G. *his arms folded*]: No "buts". We'll say no more about it. Goodbye, dear boy . . .

PAINTER: Very well! Goodbye, sir! [*He moves to the door again.*] Goodbye, sir. [*He goes out.*]

[LARGE G. *runs after him.*]

LARGE G: I say, old chap, I say. [*He goes out for a moment and comes back pulling the Painter by the sleeve.*] . . . Wait . . . after all, I'd like to do something to help you. I'll give you 400 . . .

PAINTER: 400,000 francs? Ooh!

LARGE G: Ha ha! [*Loud laughter.*]You're joking.

PAINTER *laughing too*]: You never know!

LARGE G: I'll give you 400 francs, and that's my final offer,

122

400 francs, take it or leave it.

PAINTER: All right, sir. Agreed. That's fine.

LARGE G: I was sure we'd come to an understanding. I know you artists, and you should get to know me too!

PAINTER *sincerely*]: Yes indeed!

LARGE G: I respect you, my friend.

PAINTER: Thank you, sir. You know, I should have been most upset if we'd not come to an agreement.

LARGE G: And so should I! A friendly settlement without costs is better than a long-drawn-out law-suit, however expensive.

PAINTER: I agree with you entirely.

LARGE G: You're very kind.

PAINTER: I'll unroll the picture.

LARGE G: Oh, I could have done that by myself; it's not absolutely essential. A picture is a picture. So long as it's a work of art, that's all I ask; it'll decorate the wall, liven up this gloomy room a bit, so that it won't be so unpleasant to live in . . .

PAINTER: Of course.

LARGE G: Of course.

PAINTER: Of course.

LARGE G: Using the same expression proves we're in perfect agreement.

PAINTER: Yes, the agreement is perfect.

[*They both laugh.*]

LARGE G. *back to business again*]: But perhaps we could look at the picture all the same . . . just . . . as a matter of form . . .

PAINTER: Ah?

LARGE G: It's not troubling you, I hope?

PAINTER: Oh . . . not at all . . . perhaps I am in rather a hurry . . . but then . . . for your sake . . .

LARGE G: My dear fellow, I want to know what I'm buying;

I've a right to! I don't buy anything with my eyes shut! Not even painting!

PAINTER: Fair enough; you're quite within your rights.

LARGE G: Come on then, quickly, as you say you're in a hurry.

PAINTER: Straightaway, sir. [*He unrolls his huge picture.*]

LARGE G. *as the painter unrolls the picture which trails on the floor*]: Well . . . well . . . well I never . . .

PAINTER *timidly, the picture still not quite unrolled*]: What do you think of it, sir?

LARGE G: Nothing at all just yet, dear boy. After all, I must *see* it . . . Roll it right out . . . Come along, faster, faster . . .

PAINTER: Yes sir, yes.

[*He spreads it out over the floor and gets caught up in it.*]

LARGE G. *watching him, without helping*]: You're so clumsy! Look out, don't spoil my picture!

PAINTER: I'm so sorry.

LARGE G: Oh dear oh dear oh dear . . .

PAINTER: There you are, sir, that's it . . .

LARGE G: At last!

PAINTER: What do you think of it?

LARGE G. *like a real connoisseur*]: Hmm! Well, well . . .

PAINTER: There it is.

LARGE G: It's a portrait . . . the portrait of a woman . . . Yes, that's right, it's not non-representational.

PAINTER: No.

LARGE G: Don't walk all over it then. How careless you are. I told you to look out.

PAINTER: Sorry, sir.

LARGE G. *dissatisfied*]: It's representational.

PAINTER: That's what you wanted. I told you it was.

LARGE G: We never agreed on a definition of the term. I have good taste, you know. You can trust my judgment.

Naturally I should have preferred . . . a non-representational picture, or if not, really . . . representational . . .

PAINTER: I thought you would.

LARGE G: Still, it's . . . what it is.

PAINTER: Yes, of course, it is what it is; but still, being what it is . . . what is it really? You, who have such good taste?

LARGE G: I can hardly give you a definite opinion yet, when I can't see it properly, spread out like that over the floor . . . a play is made to be acted, and a picture to be hung on the wall. On the ground it might be an ordnance survey map. You can just pick out a few details here, a few more there, a maze of lines and squiggles, the border, a few colours . . . the total effect escapes you.

PAINTER: Escapes, yes, escapes.

LARGE G: And you must realize that there's an essential difference between a mat and a Matisse, even if they do share a syllable.

PAINTER: Yes, but Matisse has got two.

LARGE G. *without moving*]: Hang it up for me; now you're here you can give me a hand.

PAINTER: Of course I will.

[*He begins to roll the picture up.*]

LARGE G: You're not going to walk off with it, are you?

PAINTER: No, sir, no. I'm re-rolling it so I can re-unroll it again on the wall. [*He makes for the back wall with the half-rolled picture.*]

LARGE G: It's just as you like, of course. You're free to do what you want.

PAINTER: Oh no, sir, I'm entirely at your service.

LARGE G: Anyway, you don't roll it up before you hang it up . . . [*Profoundly.*] I should say you'd do just the opposite.

PAINTER *right close to the wall*]: It'll have to be hung very high.

125

LARGE G: Of course it will, otherwise it'll drag on the floor. I have to tell you everything.

PAINTER: If it's to be hung very high on the wall, we'll need a ladder.

LARGE G. *calling out to the kitchen*]: Alice! Alice!

ALICE'S CRACKED VOICE: Yes. ·

[*She rushes in. She is indeed very old: her shoulders are hunched and you can see her white hair straggling over her shawl; she wears thick-rimmed dark glasses, mittens, an apron and has only one arm. She is carrying a white stick.*]

Here I am . . .

LARGE G: Well, hurry up and bring a ladder . . .

ALICE: What for?

LARGE G: Mind your own business.

ALICE: All right.

[*She goes out.*]

LARGE G: That's my sister.

PAINTER: Yes sir, I was afraid it was.

LARGE G: Hurry up, hurry up, Alice, come along . . .

[*Tapping his foot.*]

Quickly now.

ALICE: I'm coming.

[*She comes back. The first you see is the end of the ladder.*]

PAINTER: I could . . . give her a hand.

LARGE G: She needs one; then she'll have two. Why don't you help her?

ALICE *to the Painter who helps her as she struggles to carry the ladder with her one good hand and her stump*]: Thank you, sir, it's heavy and I'm tired; an old woman like me, sir, with only one arm, just think of it.

LARGE G: Always the same self-pity. The gentleman isn't interested.

[*They both carry the ladder and place it against the back wall.*]

126

ALICE: Here?

LARGE G: No, there! Mind! Go on! Be careful, don't spoil anything, don't scratch the wall. Ah! . . . Not like that . . . [*To Alice.*] Pass him the picture, pass it to him.

[*The* PAINTER *climbs the ladder and* ALICE *hands him the rolled-up picture.*]

PAINTER *trying to hang it up*]: Here, sir?

LARGE G: Wait. [*He goes to the middle of the stage, thinks for a moment, and then:*] Too high.

[*The* PAINTER *moves it from place to place, following the* LARGE GENTLEMAN's *directions, while* ALICE *flurries about in a disorganized fashion, without saying a word.*]

Too low! To the right! To the left. More to the left! No, no! . . . To the right! To the left! To the right! Too low! Too high! Too low! No! . . . It's to the right of the left, not to the left of the right. I hope it's not upside down. Hang it symmetrically. I said "symmetrically", it's very important. There, there, be careful, there! Don't move now. Fix it there and let it unroll.

[*The fixed canvas unrolls: a large picture, a kind of tapestry appears, representing a very beautiful woman, evidently royal; the back of a throne is seen; she is holding a sceptre and dressed in a crimson robe; her eyes are black.*]

Well, well . . .

ALICE: Who is it?

LARGE G: Be quiet!

PAINTER *timidly, from the top of the ladder*]: What do you think, sir?

LARGE G: I know quite well what I think, but I can't tell you a thing while you're stuck in the way, come down from the ladder, quickly, quickly.

PAINTER: Yes, sir.

[*He comes down very fast.*]

127

LARGE G: Now then, Alice, stand to one side, don't block the view, and stop putting your tongue out.

ALICE: All right, yes, all right.

LARGE G: Well, get rid of the ladder, then! You're not going to leave it there till Christmas!

PAINTER: Straightaway, sir.

LARGE G: Alice, don't waste time. Can't you help the artist move the ladder? Where's your head?

ALICE: I'm doing my best. [*She sobs.*] All the time he's scolding me, sir, if you only knew . . .

PAINTER: Oh, don't scold her, sir.

LARGE G. *to the Painter*]: It's no business of yours. [*To Alice*:] This isn't the time for tears and recriminations; it's the time for making a bargain. *Push* the ladder, then, both of you.

PAINTER: Yes, sir.

[*The* PAINTER, *and* ALICE *weeping, push the ladder aside.*]

LARGE G: That'll do!

[*Trembling, the other two stop.*]

Now let me look and decide.

[*He steps up to it, back from it and then up to it again, like a true connoisseur.*]

PAINTER: Your honest opinion . . .

LARGE G. *to Alice*]: Alice, don't stand there glued to the wall, so close to the picture. How can I see it properly? And a comparison is hardly in your favour. Turn your face to the wall.

ALICE *to the Painter*]: You see, sir, you see, I annoy him just by being here. [*She turns her back to the audience.*]

PAINTER *to Alice*]: You're making me quite upset. [*Timidly:*] You're making her quite upset, sir . . .

[ALICE *turns to face the audience, tears streaming down her face.*]

LARGE G: Alice, you're a fool!

[ALICE *weeps more loudly.*]

PAINTER: Don't cry, Madame.

LARGE G: Stick to your own affairs. You're a painter, not a comforter.

PAINTER: I beg your pardon.

LARGE G. *to Alice*]: How can I concentrate on the picture with all your tears and your nonsense? [*To the Painter:*] All day long she's crying, all day long. She spends her whole life preventing me from enjoying beauty. I've had enough of her. She's a disgrace.

PAINTER: She has no artistic impulse.

LARGE G: She's utterly devoid of any.

PAINTER: Not entirely.

ALICE *sobbing*]: What's an artistic impulse?

LARGE G: A feeling for words.

ALICE *weeping*]: A feeling for what?

LARGE G. *to the Painter*]: You see, what did I say . . .

PAINTER: Oh sir! She's more to be pitied than blamed! It's just like any other disability . . .

LARGE G: Oh dear, disabilities . . . she's got too many of them already! She's not hungry for art, that's the greatest calamity for me. That's the real reason why we don't get on together. [*To Alice:*] Get back to your pots and pans!

ALICE *wiping her eyes on her apron*]: All right, all right, all right . . .

[*She goes to the door leading to the kitchen and leaves it half open; every now and then she listens to what is being said and watches the action, sometimes coming on stage again.*]

LARGE G. *to the Painter*]: Brothers and sisters have I one . . .

PAINTER *timidly*]: Now's the time to exercise your judgment, sir.

LARGE G. *looking for a few moments in silence at the picture, while*

129

the Painter appears deeply moved]: That's just what I am exercising, dear boy . . . Hmmm . . . and not perhaps to your advantage.

PAINTER *with a forced smile*]: Never mind, sir, never mind, it can't be helped.

LARGE G: Well then . . . look here, the more I think about this piece of work of yours, the less I know what to think of it; I want to tell you exactly how it strikes me.

PAINTER: Yes, yes . . .

LARGE G: It has faults, of course, I quite see what you were trying to do, it's a portrait. The portrait of a woman, if I'm not mistaken . . .

PAINTER: No sir, indeed you're not.

LARGE G: Well . . . so it represents a woman, a seated woman . . . I'm just trying to work it out . . . sitting in a chair and holding a sceptre. It's like a big photograph: a portrait. So it must be non-representational painting. Right?

PAINTER: Exactly.

LARGE G: The chair this woman is sitting on looks very like a throne. It may even be a throne. But you can't see the lower part of it, though you can imagine how it is . . .

PAINTER: You can imagine how it is, yes, sir, at least I hope you can.

ALICE *her head appearing*]: That's the main thing, if you can imagine it.

LARGE G. *to Alice*]: Be quiet! [*To the Painter:*] She has a sceptre but no crown, so she must be a queen. The lower part you can only imagine must be the legs of this chair or throne. It's only in so far as they can be imagined, without actually being seen, that your picture can be called non-representational.

PAINTER: In that respect, yes, sir.

LARGE G: This princess, this woman, is also treated in a

130

semi-representational, semi-non-representational, style, because, although you can imagine them, you can't really see the woman's feet or legs or thighs or pelvis either.

PAINTER: Oh yes, sir, that's perfectly correct.

LARGE G: How you realized this woman *is* a woman is just one of the mysteries of the painter's art, and there I must congratulate you.

ALICE: It's by suggestion.

PAINTER: Thank you, sir.

LARGE G: Wait! The mystery must be solved. How *can* you realize it's a woman when you can only just see the top half of her bosom, the nipples being carefully, I might almost say modestly, concealed by a lace bodice. You can't see the woman's breasts, and yet you're quite sure they're there . . . The way they're suggested is very striking, unmistakable. As for her legs, you can only imagine they exist by a simple logical deduction. But they're not in any way suggested. [*Decisively.*] That's one of the faults.

PAINTER: I apologise, sir, I'm really very sorry.

LARGE G: For you see, my dear chap, art and logic are two different things, and if you have to call on logic to understand art, art in other words life, vanishes; only logic, in other words death, remains.

PAINTER: Death?

LARGE G: Yes. I mean: the death of art.

PAINTER: I follow you, sir.

LARGE G: Good.

ALICE *showing herself*]: I knew it, oh dear oh dear!

LARGE G. *to Alice*]: Mind your own business! Go away, go away!

[ALICE *disappears, only to appear again a moment later.*]

In the same way—to take another example—if to

131

understand logic, you have to call on art, logic vanishes, and nothing's left but dead art. You understand that this is only a manner of speaking, for art will live eternally. And so of course will logic. You really do understand?

PAINTER: Yes, sir. I understand you perfectly.

LARGE G: Good. This then is your weak point, the principal objection I have to make; in your work one has to imagine, and even that is not always possible, what one cannot see. There's a glaring contradiction there and consequently a confusion of styles as well: an uneasy mixture of the representational with the non-representational.

PAINTER: Yes, sir, unfortunately I see that. Your criticism is justified, but what can be done about it?

LARGE G: It's too late now . . . Perhaps you didn't allow sufficiently for this basic principle: logic works by demonstration, and art by suggestion.

PAINTER: I didn't know the principle.

LARGE G: From now on, you can think about it. After that, it's simple enough: this woman of yours, real or imaginary, representational or non-representational, is very well painted: she has brown hair, green eyes, a pale complexion, lips, nose, mouth etc . . . What's more, now I can see she's really meant to be a queen.

ALICE: Every woman's a queen for him. He sees them everywhere, at the corner of every street, street-walking queens.

[ALICE *pops her head back*.]

PAINTER: Yes, sir. She is a queen.

LARGE G: Be quiet! Don't interrupt! I want to interpret it for myself. I think I've shown myself quite capable.

PAINTER: I shan't say a word, sir.

LARGE G: Your queen is holding a sceptre, which is the perfect symbol of royalty . . . but unfortunately I notice she has no crown . . . Real or imaginary, your portrait,

132

dear boy, is incomplete . . .

PAINTER: Yes indeed. Oh, I'm really terribly sorry . . . terribly, terribly sorry . . . What can I do? [*He wrings his hands.*]

LARGE G: You should have been sorry before! There are some good qualities in your picture too, but I shall pass them over in respectful silence. In your own interest.

PAINTER: Very well.

LARGE G: To sum up, then: you need to make several essential alterations to this picture of yours. I can't take it from you in its present state.

PAINTER: Oh!

LARGE G: You can bring it back to me later. We'll discuss it another time, not now. Take it away.

PAINTER: Oh, sir . . . sir! . . . it's so awkward and heavy to carry. If you like, I'll let you have it for 300 francs.

LARGE G: Out of the question.

ALICE *snivelling in the doorway*]: Oh please, please . . . don't be so heartless, you're not being kind to him . . . he's not a kind man, sir, he's hard, he's always been hard.

LARGE G: Alice, what business is it of yours, eh? Pots and pans!

ALICE: All right, all right, I'm going, don't be cross with me. [*She disappears for a moment, then pokes her head round the door again.*]

LARGE G. *to the Painter*]: Just as a favour, my friend, I'm willing to keep it . . . for a while . . . on loan. In a month or two I'll have made up my mind whether I want to keep it for good or not. Of course I shan't be able to pay you anything.

PAINTER *falling over himself in thanks*]: Thank you, sir, thank you with all my heart. Thank you for offering to keep it here.

LARGE G: It's just as a favour.

PAINTER: I know, sir, and I'm most grateful.

LARGE G: That way, it's off your hands. Not off mine, but there . . .

PAINTER: I'm afraid not!

LARGE G: If I have the time, if I find it's worth while and your picture's capable of improvement, I'll make the necessary changes myself.

PAINTER: I'd be so grateful. How can I thank you?

LARGE G: For the loan of it, I shall ask you . . . to pay me a small sum, we'll arrange all that, dear boy, don't worry about it. I'm only doing this, because of my feeling for art and my interest in you.

PAINTER: Very generous of you, sir.

LARGE G: Unless. . . but we'll see later. If I think we could . . . make anything out of it, I'll give you a fair percentage. You're not on the telephone?

PAINTER: No, sir.

LARGE G: Oh, these artists! They're all alike!

PAINTER: I'm afraid so . . .

LARGE G: Doesn't matter . . . I've got your address. I'll write, send you a telegram. Well then . . . [*In a jocular way*:] Now I'm turning you out, you see I've work to do. Our business is settled.

PAINTER: Thank you. Goodbye, sir.

LARGE G: Our business is settled.

[*As the* PAINTER *prepares to leave,* ALICE *comes forward.*]

ALICE *to the Painter*]: Goodbye, sir, goodbye . . . look after yourself and best of luck!

[*The* LARGE GENTLEMAN *gazes at the picture; from now on he becomes more and more submissive, while* ALICE *changes her character and becomes astonishingly aggressive; as soon as the* PAINTER *leaves, the* LARGE GENTLEMAN *starts slumping and*

134

looks round-shouldered.]

LARGE G. *timidly*]: It's not bad, is it? Not bad at all, eh?

ALICE: Another of your ideas! Why do you want to buy a nasty picture like that? Funny thing to want. What came over you? You must be mad! At your age too!

LARGE G. *already weakening, but still with some trace of his former authority*]: That's my affair, I'm within my rights. After all we've got to have something on the walls, you don't understand . . . to make the place beautiful.

ALICE: Sheer snobbery . . . and we can do without *that.* Just look at it! All your haggling's a waste of time. We'll have nothing to eat, not a rag to our backs. You'll ruin us, with your stupid ideas. Better for you if you'd thought about the contract; and the paper-work; how's all that getting on, eh? Time is money.

LARGE G: Don't worry, Alice, we'll make some.

ALICE: You'd better start by seeing about the certificate.

LARGE G. *stealing a glance at the picture*]: Certificate?

ALICE: Yes. I suppose it's the first you've heard of it. I've got to go to the Town Hall about the certificate.

LARGE G: The Town Hall?

ALICE: The Town Hall. But as I've already been to the Town Hall about the certificate, it can't be about the certificate. So it must be something else. But as I've already been about something else, it can't be about that either. I wonder what it can be . . . [*The Large Gentleman is silent; Alice raises her stick.*] Eh? What's it all about? You've never given it a thought, I suppose? What do you do with your time? Waste it all gazing at her, do you? Dirty little tyke! Get on with your work!

LARGE G. *goes fearfully back to his desk, still casting furtive glances at the picture as he moves reluctantly away*]: I *am* getting on with it!

135

ALICE *pursuing the Large Gentleman, who takes refuge behind his desk*]: Snake in the grass! Boozer! You'd spend your life gazing at her! . . . Oh! My breath . . . I can't get my breath . . .

LARGE G: For goodness' sake, don't get in such a state, Alice. I promise you I'm getting on with my work!

ALICE: You always *say* that! Liar! Reptile! Good thing I'm here to keep you up to scratch!

LARGE G: I'm doing my best.

ALICE: You don't put your heart into it! *That's* all *you* think about! [*She points to the picture and raises her stick as if she were going to strike it.*]

LARGE G: Now then, Alice, my dear . . . Alice . . . it cost money, and it's going to make us some too.

ALICE *hesitating*]: Oh. I don't know what's holding me back . . . I really don't know . . . It's all *your* fault, blockhead, not the fault of that misbegotten, revolting creature over there . . .

LARGE G: Don't hit me . . . don't hit me!

ALICE: The fine gentleman wants some pictures, does he! Pictures of beautiful women . . . nude women! What do you think of that!

LARGE G. *sheltering behind the desk*]: She isn't nude, on the contrary it seems to me she's very respectably dressed.

ALICE: The way you look at her, with those piercing eyes of yours, it's just as though she hadn't a stitch on.

LARGE G: It's a useful acquisition, you don't understand.

ALICE: That's what you think, he didn't even say how much he'd pay you, for the loan.

LARGE G: He'll pay through the nose, don't you worry, it'll all be arranged . . . Meanwhile we'll both benefit from his masterpiece, yes, *you'll* benefit from it too.

ALICE: Me? Benefit from that slut! Who do you take me for?

LARGE G: I did the painter a favour, I took it off his hands, he was very pleased, it's good business, he's very grateful, he'll pay us a lot of money.

ALICE: He'll give you nothing, or hardly anything; I know artists and poets, they're not worth twopence, their sort . . . they and their tarts!

LARGE G: That's not fair.

ALICE: He was only too glad to get rid of it, no-one wants it. You'll never see him again, no flies on him, he had you on all right. You're the only one wants any of his trash . . . I'll throw it away, I will, throw it in the dustbin, into the dustbin!

LARGE G: You may think it's unwise of me to sell the golden egg before I've caught the goose . . . but I've great hopes, by Jove, yes I've great hopes . . .

ALICE: Founded on what? Meanwhile you'll spend day after day, week after week, month after month, a whole lifetime, just looking at her, wasting your time, making eyes at her, like a filthy toad . . . [*Snivelling.*] Selfish brute! Instead of looking after me, when I'm so ill, you cram the house with pictures until there's no room for more.

LARGE G: There's only one.

ALICE: A thousand too many! The house is stuffed with them! Instead of looking after me . . .

LARGE G: But I give you everything you need.

ALICE: I don't go without anything, I suppose.

LARGE G: Not as far as I can help it.

ALICE: What about my rheumatism?

LARGE G: You've got that already!

ALICE: And my broken spectacles!

LARGE G: I bought you some more. You're wearing them.

ALICE: They're not the same.

LARGE G: They're just as good.

ALICE *shouting, her stick raised*]: It's not true, you liar, you rat!

LARGE G. *lifting his eyes to Heaven*]: Will she never understand that I'm a man of high ideals!

ALICE: I'll see you don't budge from this desk! You'll stay here . . . here . . .

[*The* LARGE GENTLEMAN *sits down at his desk at the place indicated by* ALICE *with her stick.*]

Where are those contracts? Where are they?

LARGE G. *pointing to the drawer*]: They're here!

ALICE: And you leave them lying there in a drawer! Are they ready?

LARGE G: They won't take long.

ALICE: Lazy good-for-nothing! Take them out at once. What are your clients going to say? They'll all leave you everyone of them.

[*The* LARGE GENTLEMAN *takes some papers out of his drawer and sets them in front of him.*]

Get to work! You haven't even started them!

LARGE G: I have . . . just.

ALICE: There you sit, gossiping with I don't know who . . .

LARGE G: *I* didn't ask him to come!

ALICE: . . . boasting and bragging. That's all you're good for. And the painter's an idiot, an imbecile without talent, anyone could do as well, a four-year-old child would be better than that . . .

LARGE G: Children do it without thinking.

ALICE: Leaving their pictures in anyone's house, with any old snob, any old simpleton who knows nothing about it, who just pretends . . .

LARGE G: I don't pretend.

ALICE: That's worse still!

LARGE G. *timidly*]: . . . not true . . .

ALICE: Be quiet! Get on with those contracts! If they're not

138

finished this evening, no soup, no pudding, no supper. People who don't work, don't eat . . .

LARGE G. *timidly*]: It'll be finished by this evening.

ALICE: Promises! I know what *they're* worth! You'll show them to *me* when they're finished, can't trust *you*, I have to check everything, as if I'd nothing else to do . . .

LARGE G. *still timid*]: I shan't finish them if you don't leave me alone . . .

ALICE: If they're not ready, look out for yourself . . . Look out for the stick! And no supper, mind.

LARGE G. *as before*]: All right, Alice.

ALICE: I'll go and wash up your dirty dishes . . . I'll leave the kitchen door open . . . And watch yourself, that's all . . .

LARGE G: Oh, I won't . . .

ALICE: I'll have my eye on you . . . [*She points to the picture.*] And if I catch you ogling her, if I catch you . . .

LARGE G. *as before*]: I promise!

ALICE: Don't let me catch you, that's all! [*Looks at the picture and spits at it.*] I'll pay her out. You'll see what I'll do to her! [*She goes hobbling out left to the kitchen, muttering angrily; before leaving she has time to say:*] I'm watching you!

[*The* LARGE GENTLEMAN *looks at his papers and utters a sigh of relief; after a moment he wipes his brow, turns his head cautiously to take a brief glance at the picture and then bends over his papers again.*]

ALICE'S VOICE *off*]: No playing about! I'm here! Got my eye on you.

LARGE G *startled*]: No, no, Alice.

[*He goes back to work. Then another anxious glance at the kitchen door, followed by yet another; he seems reassured; he half gets up, then a little move; just at that moment the noise of breaking crockery is heard from the kitchen and* ALICE'S *voice:* "Damn". *The* LARGE GENTLEMAN *sits down again quickly, frightened out of his wits, as though the pile of dishes had been dropped on his head, and then he sets feverishly to work.*]

LARGE G: Seven and eight, fifteen; fifteen times three, forty-five; forty-five divided by three, fifteen; fifteen minus eight, seven; seven and one, eight . . . That makes eight million . . . eight million multiplied by ten, that makes eighty million . . . yes . . . eighty million, eighty million . . . eighty million . . . ten times eighty million is eight hundred million . . . a profit of eight hundred million, income tax paid . . . tax paid . . . a profit of eight hundred million . . . in two weeks that's not bad . . . it could be better . . . much better, much better!

[ALICE *can be heard snoring.*]

Is she asleep? Or is she pretending? [*Very loud.*] Eight hundred million! Eight hundred!

[ALICE *goes on snoring.*]

[*He yells out to the kitchen.*] Eight hundred million! Eight hundred mil-l-lion! [*He stops; the snoring continues.*] She's asleep . . . I've made eight hundred million, so I think I might be allowed a little amusement! [*He looks at the picture.*] An amusement that costs nothing! [*He stands up and tip-toes to the picture, then changes his mind. Cautiously he goes to the kitchen door, puts his head round and then withdraws it; meanwhile the snoring continues; he closes the kitchen door quietly so that the noise of the snoring fades and then dies away: the Large Gentleman peers through the keyhole, clamps his ear to the door and then stands erect, reassured; he goes to the middle of the stage, humming but still on tip-toe, and very cautiously as he approaches the picture; he stands in front of it, back to the public, at first with his hands folded behind him.*] A good bargain that! . . . Isn't she beautiful? I've not wasted my money! I've even made some . . . Alice can say what she likes! . . . [*He strokes the arms of the woman in the picture.*] A still queen

140

is better than a dead life! I believe I'm turning into a poet . . . turning into a poet . . . That's what I needed for inspiration . . . I'm going to be a poet, a poet . . . Hail to thee, blithe skylark. Her skin is so smooth . . . Supposing I tried, supposing I tried . . . painting can appeal to the palate too . . .

[*Smacking kisses over the portrait.*]
Darling! [*He sniffs.*] She smells nice . . . oil paint . . . [*He flattens himself against the picture.*] You're so beautiful . . . [*He steps away.*] Must keep at a distance . . . to appreciate it better . . . Good, good, good . . . it really is tremendously inspiring! To me, if not to Alice . . . And to think we have the same mother and father . . . it must have been a mistake . . . [*To the picture.*] Oh wonderful woman, so eloquent in your silence!

[*He takes a step to the left and to the right.*]
If I step to the left or the right everything changes. You look even lovelier, you're radiant from every side . . . it's all a question of perspective! It's so easy! Just change my position slightly, ever so little, as though I were dancing . . . Oh I'll learn to dance, for your sake! One step's enough, for perfect proportion. It's because one always looks at the world from the same angle that it seems so ugly, so inflexible. I'm not inflexible any more.

[*Another step to the right, then to the left; in a ridiculously pompous declamatory style.*]
The muddy waste becomes a meadow, the sky is an ocean with islands of delight . . . oases in the desert . . . rivers flowing through dry sand . . . You are a path of violets . . . You remind me of great cities engulfed by the waves . . . you remind me . . . you remind me . . . What was it, what was it? I am young again, bursting into leaf and turning green . . . well, well, well . . . I'm even blossoming . . .

141

[*He goes up to the picture and strokes the painted arms.*] I'm in flower. [*Standing sideways to the audience, he shows his rosette of the Legion of Honour, so that all can see.*] I'm in flower . . . Ah! I'm turning into a poet, I'm really becoming a poet . . .

[ALICE *pops her head in; the* LARGE GENTLEMAN *is too preoccupied to notice.*]

What do you want of me? What do you want?

ALICE: Pervert! You ought to be ashamed!

LARGE G. *completely flattened against the picture*]: Your eyes are so soft and warm they're melting me . . . [*He climbs up one or two rungs of the ladder to kiss the painted woman more easily.*]

ALICE *coming forward on to the stage; the Large Gentleman still does not see her*]: Nothing can replace the warmth of a sister's affection!

LARGE G. *as before*]: Alas, life is short and art is long!

ALICE *hobbling round in circles*]: Art is the opium of the people. So is life.

LARGE G. *coming down from the ladder*]: I shall stand back to come closer to you . . .

ALICE *as before*]: You'd better stand a long way back! [*She snivels.*] At his age too! At his age! And then she's so plain, so plain . . . she might at least be beautiful, but he's chosen the plainest!

[*The* LARGE GENTLEMAN *is blowing kisses to the picture; at the same time* ALICE *is spitting at it and threatening it with her stick.*]

What does he find so wonderful about her?

LARGE G. *esctatically*]: What do you want of me?

ALICE *as before*]: What has she got that I haven't got? I admit she's two arms, and I've only one and a half, but I *have* got legs, and she hasn't . . . And if I've lost a hand, it's only an accident of old age!

LARGE G. *as before*]: My young sovereign!

142

ALICE *as before*]: It's a trick! That picture's at least thirty years old . . .

LARGE G *as before*]: She must be about twenty, twenty for ever and ever.

ALICE *as before*]: Add that to the woman's age and it makes sixty, it makes her eighty years old, as old as I am.

LARGE G. *as before*]: And yet she lacks something . . . not much . . .

ALICE *as before*]: And if she's only twenty, he's old enough to be her father . . .

LARGE G. *as before*]: She's not quite real enough, or quite unreal . . .

ALICE *as before*]: How his imagination runs away with him! She's got nothing others haven't got, nothing at all . . . [*Snivelling to the Large Gentleman*:] You haven't even paid for her, you thief . . .

LARGE G *to Alice*]: Don't interrupt my aesthetic ecstacy with your moaning and groaning!

ALICE *to Large Gentleman*]: But she's just a make-believe queen . . . make-believe! . . . Oh dear oh dear . . . what's to become of us, he'll ruin himself because of her . . .

LARGE G *to the picture*]: I can see what you need . . .

ALICE *snivelling*]: I've a pain in my nose . . . a pain in my eyes . . .

LARGE G *happy to have made the discovery*]: I've got it . . . I'll make a few changes . . .

ALICE *snivelling*]: He doesn't think about my rheumatism . . .

LARGE G. *he goes to the drawer, opens it and takes out a crown; then he climbs the ladder again and tries in vain to put the crown on the painted woman's head.*] I'm going to crown her . . .

ALICE *as before*]: Unnecessary expense! [*To the picture.*] All because of you! Because of you! [*To the Large Gentleman.*] Selfish scoundrel!

143

LARGE G: The crown was there, in the special drawer for crowns . . . It didn't cost me anything . . . But it's expensive all the same!

ALICE: It's expensive all the same!

LARGE G. *climbing the ladder*]: That's it, just the thing . . .

ALICE: What a silly idea! Oh dear oh dear . . . old devil, he only thinks of his own amusement, never of other people's . . .

[*The* LARGE GENTLEMAN *tries in vain to fix the crown on the painted woman's head.*]

LARGE G: Oh dear, it won't stick, it won't fix on!

ALICE: I told you you couldn't, you're too old for that now . . .

LARGE G. *persisting*]: It won't fix . . .

ALICE: Cranky ideas! It's terrible!

LARGE G. *in despair*]: I didn't start painting soon enough . . . And now it's too late.

ALICE: What a way to spend his time! And all for that idiot!

LARGE G. *on the ladder*]:.Let's try something else . . .

ALICE *weeping*]: Oh dear oh dear!

LARGE G. *at the picture*]: Try and hold it in your arms, then . . . [*He tries to put the crown in the woman's arms, but of course does not succeed.*] I can't do it! She doesn't want it! [*He starts snivelling too*].

ALICE *as before*]: Serve you right!

LARGE G. *as before*]: It's such a shame!

ALICE *as before*]: That'll teach you!

LARGE G. *as before, to Alice*]: Well why don't you help me?

ALICE: You expect *me* to help! What sauce!

[*While the* LARGE GENTLEMAN *still tries in vain to fit the crown on the picture,* ALICE, *in tears, goes into the kitchen, or to the corner of the room, to fetch a pail of water. Coming back with the pail she throws the contents over the* LARGE GENTLE-MAN'S *shoulders.*]

Take that! Casanova!

LARGE G. *caught by surprise, drops the crown on the floor*]: You're going too far, Alice! [*He comes down from the ladder.*] Alice, what did you do that for? [*After shaking himself like a poodle, he glares threateningly at her.*]

ALICE: I feel ill! Oh, I'm going to faint! I've a pain in my head, I want to be sick! I can't stand up, I'm going to fall! . . . going to fall! go and fetch a chair, what are you doing! You'd be better off buying chairs, they're more useful than pictures.

LARGE G: All right . . . all right . . .

ALICE: Take the pail with you!

LARGE G: Yes . . . yes . . .

[*He picks up the pail and casts a glance at the picture.*] She's so beautiful, even without a crown!

ALICE *snivelling*]: I'm going to fall . . . Hurry up.

LARGE G: Oh . . . I shall never have any peace . . . never be myself! [*He makes reluctantly for the kitchen, carrying the pail, and as he disappears he is heard saying:*] Never be myself!

ALICE *straightening herself up, while the Large Gentleman is off stage, and facing the picture.*] Loathsome creature! [*She threatens it.*]

LARGE G. *coming back with an armchair that has a fairly high back.*] Here! Sit down! [*He sets the chair down to the right of the picture.*]

ALICE: Not next to her! Not next to her! [*She sits down all the same.*]

LARGE G: It's only because the comparison's not in your favour! [*In the hand he is holding behind his back, it can now be seen he is carrying a pistol.*]

ALICE: What impertinence! You've never used your eyes properly, never looked at me! You don't know how to! It's a bad picture, a baby could do better!

145

[*She gets up and hobbles about, striking the floor with her stick.*]

LARGE G. *sweetly*]: You've a blind man's stick and you use it as though you were deaf!

ALICE *as before*]: All right, I can hear you, hear you quite clearly, thank you!

LARGE G. *still more sweetly*]: Sit down . . . you're tired . . . rest a bit! Here's the chair!

ALICE *as before*]: What are you fussing about the chair for? Leave things where they are. You turn everything upside down.

LARGE G *as before*]: You were about to faint . . . sit down and you'll feel better.

ALICE *as before*]: I haven't the time. And I've things to do. I'll work till I drop, like a horse . . .

LARGE G *suddenly very harsh*]: Don't move.

ALICE *as before*]: You needn't think you can stop me.

[*The* LARGE GENTLEMAN *points the pistol at her.*]
Ah! Murderer! Murderer! [*Sits down, terrified.*] He's got a pistol! Murderer!

LARGE G: Didn't the doctor say you must have rest?

ALICE *trembling in front of the pistol*]: Why don't you send me away to the mountains?

LARGE G: I haven't any mountains to hand. I've nothing but a pistol.

ALICE: Your finger might slip on the trigger.

LARGE G: You can slip in the mountains too! Keep quite still . . . And it's my finger, not yours.

ALICE: What's wrong with you . . . Tell me . . . Say something . . . you're my brother . . . it's only words that are important, all the rest is nonsense.

LARGE G: For me it's the opposite! Keep quiet . . . Don't move . . . I don't want you to speak or move again, without my permission! [*Pointing the pistol at her.*] Careful now!

ALICE *snivelling*]: Oh . . . accidents happen so quickly . . .

LARGE G: Exactly. Stop crying. Not allowed!

ALICE: Why are you frightening your sister like this? Why do you want to kill her?

LARGE G: That's my affair!

ALICE: I'm sorry . . . I'm sorry . . . [*At a sudden movement of her head, her shawl falls back revealing her grey, dirty, unkempt hair.*] Now my shawl's fallen on the floor . . . Look what you've done! Let me pick it up!

LARGE G: Not my fault. Leave it alone or I warn you, this'll go off . . .

ALICE: I haven't got another one . . . I'm cold . . . It'll get dirty! [*She starts to pick it up.*]

LARGE G: No! No cheating!

ALICE: Stop playing with that pistol!

LARGE G: Not allowed to move or cry, be careful, it's loaded.

ALICE: I shan't move or speak again, don't fire, brother dear . . . I'm not cheating . . .

LARGE G: Sit up straight . . . lean against the back of the chair.

ALICE: It hurts me, I can't!

LARGE G: There's no such word as can't . . . Bend your knees . . . go on . . . go on . .

[ALICE, *terrified, obeys painfully.*]

ALICE: My rheumatism . . .

LARGE G. *playing dangerously with the pistol*]: I don't want to hear . . . go on, go on!

ALICE: With that pistol, if you're not careful, you might kill the neighbours' birds!

LARGE G: A lot I care! [*He sticks the pistol under Alice's nose.*] Lay your arm along the arm of the chair. [*She hesitates and pulls a face.*] Look sharp, get a move on! Keep still and not a word!

ALICE: An old woman like me, your sister who's always spoilt you and now you want to kill me . . . if you've no pity for me, remember my age!

LARGE G: For the last time, be quiet! You're too old to talk! Look out! [*He brandishes the pistol.*] Lose your temper and it'll go off! Come on, your arm along the arm of the chair, one on top of the other . . . Do you hear? [*She obeys, trembling.*] An excellent target!

ALICE: Ooh!

LARGE G: Remember the pistol, it's loaded! Head up, head on high . . .

[ALICE *tries to speak.*]

Ssh! Dear oh dear!

[*Tapping with his foot.*]

Not one movement . . . Smile! Smile, can't you!

[*He holds the pistol against her cheek.* ALICE *smiles and keeps this fixed smile to the end. He moves away a little, after having roughly snatched off* ALICE's *second shawl, which he throws over her knees.*]

Ready now! I'm going to fire! [*A shot.*]

ALICE: Ah!

[ALICE *has a low-cut dress and we can now see that her bosom is the same as that of the woman in the picture. As she moves in her fright, her white wig and her spectacles fall off; we can see she has brown hair, her face and her eyes are exactly like those of the painted woman.*]

LARGE G: Well! Well! Well!

[*At this moment an arm grows on* ALICE's *stump.*]

And there's her arm too!

[*According to the production, it could be only at this moment that* ALICE *takes off her spectacles with her new-found hand. Spectacles, wig, etc. lie on the floor, all that remains of the dead.*]

Hurrah! Hurrah!

[*He fires the pistol into the air.*]

My idea was an inspiration, a wonderful inspiration! [*He jumps for joy, then stops.*] And the sceptre!

[*And now* ALICE's *white stick becomes luminous; if this effect is difficult to realize, the* LARGE GENTELMAN *can throw* ALICE's *stick aside and place in her hand a sceptre he has taken from the drawer; to make the stick luminous it only needs an electric light bulb at the end—*ALICE *is radiant.*]

And there's the sceptre! Bravo! Bravo! Master painter, I congratulate you! [*He shakes himself by the hand.*] Now she needs the crown! [*He sets the crown on* ALICE's *head. It is luminous too*] It's a masterpiece! I've created a master-piece! [*He sobs for joy as he gazes at her.*] I could weep for joy. She outshines the model! I've improved on the painter. Don't need him any more! Want no more of his pictures! I can make them myself . . . and better ones! I shall found an Academy of Beauty! [*He bows grotesquely to the picture and to the lovely motionless Alice.*] Your Majesty! Your Majesty! Without a crown! And crowned! Your Majesty! Your Majesty! [*Then, to the audience.*] I am perfect! I was right!

[*The door on the right opens and the neighbour appears, she is exactly like* ALICE *before her transformation.*]

NEIGHBOUR *coming in with a chair*]: Oh, I beg your pardon!

[*The* LARGE GENTLEMAN, *slightly embarrassed, breaks off.*]

Am I disturbing you?

LARGE G: Oh no! . . . well in fact, no . . . I was jumping about like that, because I was happy . . .

NEIGHBOUR: I brought my knitting along, and my chair too, because I know you haven't any to spare in your place . . . it's cold at home . . . and it's not much warmer here . . . I don't want to be a nuisance.

149

LARGE G: Why don't you come in, then?

[*This conversation has taken place by the door; the* NEIGHBOUR *now comes into the room.*]

NEIGHBOUR *seeing Alice*]: So you've been buying statues of queens! Beautifying the home!

LARGE G: As you see!

NEIGHBOUR: And a picture too? It looks as if it was copied from the statue . . . without the crown . . .

LARGE G. *with a burst of gratified laughter.*] Just the opposite . . . it's the statue that's a copy of the picture, or rather an improvement on it, with the crown added . . .

NEIGHBOUR: Oh yes . . . it's better than the model . . . it's magnificent!

LARGE G: I'm an artist!

NEIGHBOUR: . . . there's more weight about it, more flesh . . . I never knew you were such a genius! My congratulations!

LARGE G: Never judge by appearances again . . .

NEIGHBOUR: You'd think she was alive. She's beautiful.

LARGE G: Ha! Ha! Ha! It's Alice!

NEIGHBOUR: It can't be . . . Oh please do the same for me . . .

LARGE G: It's hard work. It costs money.

NEIGHBOUR: I'd give you my last farthing.

LARGE G: Very well. When you appeal to me like that, I give way. [*Aside.*] I'll get hundreds of thousands, when I sell her! [*To the Neighbour.*] Put your chair there, sit down and do as I say, like this.

[ALICE *and the* NEIGHBOUR *are on either side of the picture.*] We'll start!

[*He takes out his pistol.*]

NEIGHBOUR: Oh . . . a paint gun, I love *them* . . .

LARGE G: Now you must sit quite still . . .

[*The* NEIGHBOUR *sits motionless on the chair.*] We start . . .

150

[*The door on the right opens and the* PAINTER *appears.*]

PAINTER: Good morning, sir!

LARGE G: What do you want?

PAINTER *still shy*]: I'm sorry, sir. You told me to come back in three weeks' time, to know if you're taking my picture . . . if you decide . . .

LARGE G: Why don't you look and see what I've done!

PAINTER: Ooh! . . . it's marvellous . . .

LARGE G: My sister . . .

PAINTER: It can't be . . . she looks wise and beautiful, like a goddess!

LARGE G: I undertook to re-educate her! Sometimes by fear, sometimes by persuasion . . .

PAINTER: By fear!

LARGE G. *showing the pistol*]: With this. [*He puts the pistol to his temple.*]

PAINTER: Oh . . . please . . . don't do that . . . you'll do something dreadful . . .

LARGE G: No I won't . . .

[*He fires a shot.*]

PAINTER: Aah! Sir!

LARGE G. *laughing*]: I told you it wasn't dangerous . . . it's just to frighten you . . . you see, I've done better than you . . .

PAINTER: Oh much better, sir . . . it's true you told me you had talent, but I never believed you had as much as this . . . such an achievement, you know, reveals the touch of a master, rather than beginners' luck! . . . But what am I going to do?

LARGE G: *I*'ve become an artist. *You* must be a business man!

PAINTER *in despair*]: The only thing left for me to do is to take my picture down!

LARGE G: First, you must give me forty million for the loan.

151

PAINTER: I haven't such a large sum on me!

LARGE G: You can pay it in instalments . . . In forty days, a million a day . . . and ten million interest!

PAINTER: Yes, sir, that's reasonable! Meanwhile I'll leave it with you . . .

LARGE G: That'll be eighty million! . . . Agreed. You may go.

PAINTER *about to go*]: Goodbye, sir. I really do admire you. [*He stops on his way to the door. Very foolishly:*] You had one twin sister before, now you've two twin sisters; with this lady you'll have three twin sisters.

[*During this time the* LARGE GENTLEMAN *has taken two other crowns from the desk drawer.*]

LARGE G. *putting one crown on the Neighbour's head, and the other on his own*]: And I'll make the fourth!

PAINTER: Well really!

LARGE G: Let me get on with my work!

[*Pistol shots into the air, fire crackers and flashing lights.*]

CURTAIN

ANGER

A Film Scenario

ANGER

The first shot is of a spring sky; while a peal of bells rings out a little church comes into view and the camera travels slowly down from top to bottom. The clock says twelve mid-day. Then, by the church, you can see the small square of a typical country town. There is quite a pause between each chime and, to begin with, everything progresses at a very slow pace. People are coming out of church, all serene and smiling, nodding amicably to each other and politely exchanging formal greetings of great gentility. The old ladies are coming out of church. One of them walks past the traditional beggar and gives him a coin: "Here's something for Sunday, my good man." "God bless your kind heart, Madam," replies the beggar, smiling broadly. The lady moves on and the beggar says, with a beatific smile: "Begging's a pleasant occupation, when there are such charitable folk around." One lady to another: "Hello, dear, how's your poor husband?" She replies: "He's happy now. He's got used to being paralysed." People are still strolling about, elaborately doffing their hats and exchanging affectionate waves of the hand. Some trees are seen, the roofs of the houses shining in the sun, and windows that reflect the light. At one of the windows, a woman in her Sunday-best is calling to a young lad below, who has just come out of the house. "Don't forget to buy some flowers for Auntie," she says. The boy replies: "No, mother, I won't forget, and I'll give her your love." If you like, two or three other edifying scenes of a similar nature can be included.

155

More of the square is discovered and a small café is seen. A respectable country gentleman is sitting at one of the tables on the terrace with his wife; another couple of the same age are at another table. The first gentleman says to the second: "You see, on Sundays I only drink mineral water. Alcohol is for weekdays." The second gentleman: "With me it's the other way round."

A little boy walks by with his grandmother. He is patted on the head and offered sweets. The little boy: "Thank you, Madame." His grandmother says to the lady who has offered the child the sweets: "You can offer him a sweet, Madame, he's a good little boy, he doesn't pick his nose." The little boy: "I've got the badge of honour," and he shows off his good conduct badge while the grown-ups stand around him and titter. "My grandson's very clever. He wants to go to grammar school." One of the gentlemen: "Which grammar school?" The grandmother: "Well . . . to a superior grammar school." One of the four actors playing the couples could have a little dog and another a little cat. The dog sits up and begs, the cat arches its back and purrs; the two animals make a touching sight; their masters are enchanted: "Aren't they sweet!" The lady who owns the dog: "Your cat's even more gentle than my dog." The gentleman with the cat: "He's never scratched anybody." The owner of the dog: "He's never bitten anybody." The gentleman who owns the cat: "Oh! These little animals, you know!" The lady who owns the dog: "They can do everything but speak." The lady who owns the cat: "You're quite right." The gentleman who owns the dog: "They understand everything."

Other happy scenes follow: the priest goes by on his way from the church. A gentleman calls to him: "Good-day, Father."

The priest replies: "Good-day, Schoolmaster." The tramp who appeared earlier affectionately greets the gendarme who returns an equally friendly greeting. "How are you, my dear chap? Have you found somewhere to stay?" The tramp: "I'm all right, thanks. There's a dear old soul who's putting me up." The gendarme: "Plenty of dear old souls around!" The tramp: "Plenty of them, I'm glad to say!" The gendarme: "Plenty, I'm glad to say . . . . When you get bored, come and see me at the station."

The camera moves to the interior of a pastry shop. A young husband is holding in one hand a little box of cakes which he has just bought, and in the other some flowers. The young husband to the lady behind the counter: "My wife loves cakes, she adores strawberry tarts." The lady: "You *are* an attentive husband. You must be very fond of each other." The young husband: "I'm in a hurry, she's expecting me. I mustn't keep her waiting." He goes out of the shop. In the square he waves to his young wife who is at a window in the building opposite. They blow kisses to each other. Happily, he makes his way home. There could be other people carrying cakes and going into various houses. The young husband enters his house. His wife opens the door. The young husband: "Hello, darling!" The young wife: "Hello, darling! What, another surprise!" He gives her the flowers. She kisses him. Then the cakes. She kisses him. The young wife puts the cakes down on the table, which is set for lunch, and puts the flowers in a vase. He takes off his boater, gives it to her, and they kiss. She goes and puts all these things away. The interior of the house is shown. It is simple, pleasant and very bright: the furniture and wallpaper very light in colour, and a television set with the news on. He asks: "What's the news?" She: "Good, of course, as usual."

157

The lady television annoucer: "The gathering of all the Heads of State culminated in a banquet to follow the general reconciliation. After the speeches the Heads of State embraced one another." A brief shot of the Heads of State does, in fact, show them embracing and saying to one another: "We agree to everything you ask." The young husband: "That's good! Every day for three years now they've been having reconciliations."

A brief love scene between the young married couple. They kiss as they murmur to each other; "my dove, my pigeon, my rabbit, my lamb, my little pussy cat, my partridge, my chicken, my squirrel, my honeybunch, my flower, my little cough-drop."

Just after the young husband arrives home, a few short sequences could be introduced to show an elderly gentleman, also with some flowers, going into another apartment in the same block of flats. When the young husband has taken off his jacket, there could be a shot of another gentleman in another apartment, taking off his jacket and handing it to his wife. And another couple too: a bearded Greek Orthodox priest who is kissing his wife. Finally, in the apartment of yet another couple, the gentleman is asking: "What's the news?" Obviously this question should be put immediately after the question asked by the young husband. The love scene between the young couple is interspersed with sequences showing identical love scenes on every floor of the building: so that after the young husband has said, "my dove" it's the wife of the bearded priest you can see and hear calling her husband "my treasure." After "my pigeon," it's a little old man you can see and hear calling his great fat wife "my little flea," and so on, and so on . . .

158

The young wife: "We'll have another kiss later on, it's time to eat now . . ." The young husband: "Yes, I'm hungry." She takes off her little apron and goes to hang it up; he follows her and they kiss. He goes to the table and sits down, then gets up again several times to go and kiss her. The young wife: "Now, behave yourself! I don't want you to die of hunger." This shot and the same remark are repeated in two or three other apartments with the other couples. The young wife: "Look, I've got a present for you too!" She brings him a tie. The young husband: "Oh, isn't it lovely!" He puts on his new tie. The young wife: "It'll go nicely with your jacket." He puts his jacket on. They kiss, words of endearment. He goes over to the mirror, puts on his boater and studies himself. "It suits me very well." He kisses her. The young wife: "Lunch is ready, darling." They go to the table and sit down. The young wife: "You're not going to sit at table with your hat on!" The young husband: "I'm sorry." He takes off his hat and gives it to her; she gets up and puts it away. He takes off his jacket and gives it to her; she goes and puts it away. He looks as if he's going to take off his tie, then he changes his mind: "No, it's too nice, I'll keep it on." This last remark can be made by several husbands in the building.

The young couple are, at last, ready to start their meal. Close-up of the young wife's hands lifting a soup-tureen and putting it on the table. The young husband pulls a face and says: "Soup again!" By superimposing and cross-fading a series of shots, various hands and soup-tureens are seen, belonging, as it seems, to different families in the building.

The young wife: "You don't have it in the week, that's why I make it for you on Sundays. It's a summer soup." The young husband: "How thoughtful of you." The young husband is about to take his first spoonful when he sees an enormous fly floating in his soup-plate. The young man frowns; his young wife looks worried: "Something's wrong. What's the matter?" The young man, still good-humouredly: "It's nothing, nothing unusual, I'm used to it . . . A fly in the soup. Just like every other Sunday." The young wife: "A fly in the soup? Liar!" Young husband: "What's that, if it's not a fly?" Young wife: "You put it there to annoy me." "Now look here, darling, you don't really believe that, it's stupid." Young wife: "That's no reason to insult me!" Young husband: "I'm not insulting you."

Further sequences show us different husbands realising that there is a fly in their respective bowls of soup. "A fly," they say: (First the bearded priest; then another wife in response to another husband: "What fly?" The bearded priest: "Look!") In another apartment a judge sitting at table: "Every Sunday, for thirty years, I've been finding . . ." Another shot of the teacher saying to his wife: "A fly in my soup!" The local priest is seen remarking to his maid: "I mean to say . . ." In the dog-owners' apartment, the husband says: "Every Sunday now, for twenty-five years!" In the apartment of the great fat lady: "His Lordship's gone all finicky, has he!"

Back in the apartment of the young married couple, the young wife says: "What a fuss about a fly! His Lordship's gone all finicky, has he! You weren't brought up in a palace, anyway. I know what your parents were." Young husband: "What were they?" Young wife: "Rag-and-bone merchants." Young husband: "They're retired now, and besides, you shouldn't look down on any job. Leave my

160

parents alone!" Young wife: "What have I done to them?" Young husband: "I'd rather be a rag-and-bone man than a pimp." Young wife: "And who are you calling pimp, if you please?" "Your father, everyone knows about it. Because he was a failure as a rag-and-bone man. It's a tough career, the rag-and-bone trade. Tough because it's honest!" Young wife: "You ought to be ashamed, to be so rude about my parents! You should be grateful to them. What would have become of you, good-for-nothing, if it weren't for the dowry they gave us?" Young husband: "They were forged notes they gave me. I had to sell them at half the price." Young wife: "It came to a pretty packet all the same." Young husband: "That's no reason anyway, why you should deliberately put flies in my soup every Sunday." Young wife: "They warned me, you know. They told me not to marry you. They said you were mad as a hatter. He was dead right, my uncle was. I ought to have listened to him." Young husband: "That old imbecile! He was always half dotty." Young wife: "Not half so dotty as your cousin, she was the village idiot!"

More sequences in other apartments follow: the wife of the bearded priest says: "You and your *aunt!*" Then the judge says to his wife: "Your half-witted great-grandfather!" The judge's wife replies: "You and your family of gallows-birds!" The local priest says to his house-keeper: "A family of heathens!" In another apartment the tramp says to the old lady: "Imposters! Faked-up gentry, lady, that's what you've all been." At the dog-owners' the wife can be seen pointing at her husband and saying to her dog: "Bite him, boy!" At the cat-owners' the cat is seen hurling itself at the wife.

Back at the young couple's the husband tips the contents of the soup-tureen over his wife's head. Similar sequences

161

follow in rapid succession in the other apartments. Then soup starts seeping out from under the doors of all the apartments and forms a torrent, which pours down the stairs. Inevitably, the couples come to blows. The wives take up the challenge. Half-a-dozen hands slap half-a-dozen faces belonging to their respective husbands.

In the young couple's apartment, the wife calls her husband: "Murderer!" In every household people start flinging crockery about. One of the plates thrown by one of the husbands or one of the wives falls at the feet of a police sergeant; he hardly has time to look round before another plate crashes at his feet, and another; then one hits him on the head, and he blows his whistle to call for help from his colleagues. Another shot shows us a duster that falls on a hot-plate and starts to burn: this starts a fire in the building.

From now on shot follows shot in very rapid succession. Inside the apartments the married couples are brawling and breaking china etc. Some of them are violently flung out on the landing, and everyone starts fighting anybody, while the soup goes flooding down the stairs.

The police arrive in their vans. From their windows the various families see them coming. At one window a husband, between blows, shouts: "The cops!" Then one of the wives cries: "The cops!"

The police pour out of several vans and run into the houses. They soon come out again, dragging with them furious husbands who are struggling and shouting: "Help! The cops!" The building is in flames, the firemen arrive as well, and the townsfolk turn out to defend those who have been arrested.

The scuffle between the police and the local population spreads to the whole district. For this the archives of the cinema can be consulted for pictures of riots: the tanks used in Berlin against the workers, for example, or the skirmishing between Blacks and Whites in South Africa and such like. In one apartment we see the burning duster, which has sent the whole building up in flames. Other shots are of firemen arriving and trying to put out blazing infernos: these can also be found in the archives. Then there will be pictures of war: Poincaré and Clemenceau inspecting the troops, Hitler or Mussolini haranguing the crowds, the bombing of London or Hamburg. Then all hell breaks loose, with floods and earthquakes etc., which finally lead to a shot of the atom bomb exploding.

This little film is centred around two characters who appear at the crucial moments in the action. The Lone Gentleman and the Lady Television Announcer, who are seen, one or other of them, at regular intervals. The Gentleman is sitting at a table in a café. Calm at the outset, he gradually becomes angry all by himself. As the riot gets worse, so does his temper, which is a mute reflection of the brawling. Before the planet explodes, so does his face, which has already turned puce. The other character, the Lady Television Announcer, appears from time to time, calm and smiling, on a television screen, then across the whole cinema screen, to make announcements that have nothing to do with the action. She talks about springtime, and brooks, and flowers, and meadows. When the Gentleman's head has exploded, just before the

163

planet blows up, she makes the following announcement, smiling her most ravishing smile and revealing her beautiful teeth: "Ladies and gentlemen, in a few minutes you can see the end of the world."

Final shot: the planet exploding.

December 1961.

This scenario was used in the film *The Seven Deadly Sins*, in which it figured as one of the sketches.

SALUTATIONS

CHARACTERS

FIRST GENTLEMAN

SECOND GENTLEMAN

THIRD GENTLEMAN

LADY SPECTATOR

LADY SPECTATOR'S NEIGHBOUR

THIRD SPECTATOR

SALUTATIONS

1st GENTLEMAN *seeing the 2nd and 3rd Gentlemen as he comes in*]:
Good-morning, Gentlemen!

2nd GENTLEMAN *seeing the 1st and 3rd Gentlemen as he comes in*]:
Good-morning, Gentlemen!

3rd GENTLEMAN *seeing the 1st and 2nd Gentlemen as he comes in*]:
Good-morning, Gentlemen!

1st GENTLEMAN *to the 2nd*]: Glad to see you. How are things
going?

2nd GENTLEMAN *to the 1st*]: Fine, thanks. And you?

3rd GENTLEMAN *to the 1st*]: How are things going?

1st GENTLEMAN *to the 3rd*]: Warmly. And you? [*To the 2nd*:]
Coldly. And you?

3rd GENTLEMAN *to the 1st*]: Nicely. And you?

2nd GENTLEMAN *to the 3rd*]: Nastily. And you?

1st and 2nd *to the 3rd*]: And you?

3rd GENTLEMAN: Peculiarly. And you?

2nd GENTLEMAN *to the 3rd*]: Melancholically. And you?

1st GENTLEMAN *to the 2nd*]: Earlymorningishly. And you?

2nd GENTLEMAN *to the 3rd*]: Gloamingly. And you?

3rd GENTLEMAN *to the 1st*]: Obesely. And you?

1st GENTLEMAN *to the 2nd*]: Acephallically. And you?

2nd GENTLEMAN *to the 3rd*]: Agnostically. And you?

3rd GENTLEMAN *to the 1st*]: Amphibiously. And you?

1st GENTLEMAN *to the 2nd*]: Theoretically. And you?

2nd GENTLEMAN *to the 3rd*]: Practically. And you?

3rd GENTLEMAN *to the 1st*]: Abstractly. And you?

1st GENTLEMAN *to the 2nd*]: Concretely. And you?

2nd GENTLEMAN *to the 3rd*]: Apoplectically. And you?

3rd GENTLEMAN *to the 1st*]: Anaemically. And you?
[*Silence. Members of the audience start coughing. Suddenly, the 1st and 2nd* GENTLEMEN *address the 3rd* GENTLEMAN:]
1st and 2nd *to the 3rd*]: And you? and you?
[*During the following speeches the 1st and 2nd* GENTLEMEN *go on asking the 3rd* GENTLEMAN: *"And you? And you? And you?" at a gradually increasing tempo; as for the 3rd* GENTLEMAN, *he turns his head, faster and faster, towards the 1st and 2nd* GENTLEMEN *alternately, illustrating as best he can by means of appropriate gestures the meaning of each word he utters.*]

3rd GENTLEMAN: Getting on . . . Adolescently, arthritically, asteroidically, astrolabically, atrabiliously, balalaikally, baobabically, barometrically, bisextilically, cacophonically, callipygically, caniculishly, cantileverishly, carabinaciously, carcassonically, carthaginically, cataclinically . . .

LADY SPECTATOR *from the audience*]: It's all in verse! . . .

3rd GENTLEMAN *continuing*]:
catamaranishly, cataplasmically, charivaraciously . . .

THE LADY SPECTATOR'S NEIGHBOUR *in a stage whisper to her*]: Anyone could do that!

3rd GENTLEMAN *continuing*]:
chipolatoically, choleranically, circumlocutionally, cirrhosisically,

clairvoyantically . . .

3rd SPECTATOR *from the audience, to the Lady Spectator's neighbour*]: You try it then. It's not so easy!

3rd GENTLEMAN *continuing*]:
concatenatiously,
concupiscently,
crepitatiously,
cucurbitaciously,
decrepitatiously,
deflagratiously . . .

1st SPECTATOR *from the audience*]: All you need is a dictionary!

3rd SPECTATOR: There's no harm in that—dictionaries have all the words.

2nd SPECTATOR: Even the word dictionary!

3rd GENTLEMAN: deliquescently,
diarrhoetically,
diastetically,
dichotocomically,
diuretically,
dodecahedronically,
draconically,
ectoplastically . . .

LADY SPECTATOR *from the audience*]: It's not so easy for the actor!

3rd GENTLEMAN: . . . empathetically,
endosmotically,
eructatiously,
epidiascopically,
euphorically,
ecstatically,
phantasmagorically . . .

1st SPECTATOR *from the audience*]: It's an excuse for an actor to show off!

LADY SPECTATOR: He's very good at miming!

2nd GENTLEMAN *taking over from the 3rd Gentleman, while the 1st and 3rd Gentlemen go on asking him: And you? And you? And you?*]:
Farinaceously,
feculantly,
fictitiously,
finically,
phlegmatically,
flagrantly,
florescently,
formidamnably . . .

THE THREE SPECTATORS: Oh! . . . He's on form!

[*Now it is the* 1st GENTLEMAN'S *turn:*]

1st GENTLEMAN: . . . fortunately,
fougassically,
fructiferously,
frenetically,
funereally,
furfuraceously,
gagarifically,
gallivantageously,
gallinaceously,
gallophobically,
ganglionically,
gangrievously,
garibaldically,
gastronomically,
gastralgically . . .

[*Then suddenly the* 1st GENTLEMAN *turns towards the* 2nd GENTLEMAN:*]

1st GENTLEMAN: And you? [*The pace slows down.*]

2nd GENTLEMAN: Gasteropodically . . . [*To the 3rd:*] And you?

170

3rd GENTLEMAN: Genealogically . . . [*To the 1st*:] And you?

LADY SPECTATOR *from the audience*]: But the words are quite well chosen! . . .

1st GENTLEMAN: Genitally! . . . [*To the 2nd*:] And you?

1st SPECTATOR *in the audience, to the Lady Spectator*]: They're not, you know!

2nd GENTLEMAN: Genetically. [*To the 3rd*:] And you?

3rd GENTLEMAN: Glycerinically. [*To the 1st*:] And you?

2nd SPECTATOR *to the 1st Spectator, in the audience*]: Well, what more do you want?

1st GENTLEMAN: Gonococcically. [*To the 2nd*:] And you?

2nd GENTLEMAN: Gymnosophically. [*To the 3rd*:] And you?

3rd GENTLEMAN: Gyroscopically. [*To the 1st*:] And you?

1st GENTLEMAN: Harmoniously. Very harmoniously. [*To the 2nd*:] And you?

[*The tempo increases again.*]

1st GENTLEMAN *to the 3rd*]: And you?

3rd GENTLEMAN *to the 1st*]: And you?

1st GENTLEMAN *to the 2nd*]: And you?

2nd GENTLEMAN *to the 3rd*]: And you?

3rd GENTLEMAN *to the 1st*]: And you?

1st GENTLEMAN *to the 2nd*]: And you?

2nd GENTLEMAN *to the 3rd*]: And you?

3rd GENTLEMAN *to the 1st*]: And you?

1st GENTLEMAN *to the 2nd*]: And you?

2nd GENTLEMAN *to the 3rd*]: And you?

3rd GENTLEMAN *to the 1st*]: And you?

1st GENTLEMAN *to the 2nd*]: And you?

[*The three characters separate. Each one on his own, with a finger pointing at his own chest, asks himself:*]

ALL THREE GENTLEMEN:

And you? And you? And you?
And you? And you? And you?

171

And you? And you? And you?
And you? And you? And you?
And you? And you? And you?
And you? And you? And you?
[*Among the audience, the* SPECTATORS *rise to their feet.*]

THE THREE SPECTATORS:
And us? And us? And us? And us? And us? And us?

THE THREE GENTLEMEN and THE THREE SPECTATORS together:
And how are things with us?
How are things with us?
[*Pause.*]

1ST GENTLEMAN: Things are going famously, we're getting on ionescoically!

The fourth spectator, who does not exist: I knew it! That was bound to be the last word.

CURTAIN

Paris, 1950.